THE GIRL
OF
MY DREAMS

ANTONIO DEMARCO

PAGE PUBLISHING, INC.
Conneaut Lake, PA

First originally published by Page Publishing 2020

ISBN 978-1-6624-0374-3 (pbk)
ISBN 978-1-6624-0375-0 (digital)

Printed in the United States of America

ONE

Where does love live, in our hearts, in our minds, or somewhere else? Does love seek us out when we are lost or abandon us when it's necessary? Is love everything we have been led to believe, or is it something we only dream about?

I t is a day unlike any other day and winter is well underway in the sleepy little town of Grantsville, New Mexico. The mornings are still a chilly thirty-five degrees on 1065 San Jose Drive, a Mayberry type of street where some of the roads are still dirt. This year was unusually cold, a lingering kind of winter that just sort of hung around as if it had nowhere else to go and was in no particular hurry to get there.

Ryan Allen rolls down the window just enough to toss out what was left of a lit cigarette; there are no power windows on the old 1976 pickup, the old hand cranks are still cold to the touch, but Ryan didn't mind, after all the truck was a gift from his father who bought the truck brand new when Ryan was still a boy. Ryan can still remember even at age ten years old the fierce and tense negotiation between the salesman and his father, who was not afraid to take the fight to them he thinks, laughing aloud. In that case the sale of the truck hinged on a difference of twenty five dollars, to which obviously his father was victorious. The wind from the open window blows bits of ash back into the truck like small flakes of gray snow. Ryan brushes the ashes off of the seat and his jacket, just in time to catch a glimpse of the bright glow of the cigarette coal quickly flying from the end of the cigarette and bounce off the pavement.

Ryan is proud of the fact that he has cut down on smoking, a smirk on his face as he can hear his wife's voice in his head, "You have got to quit smoking." However a grin and a little laugh overtake the smirk, *I will never quit*, Ryan whispers to himself. As he drives along the familiar road with little else to do but listen to the radio, he ponders as to what his day would look like and what it would have in store for him. He thinks of the long hours of his workday still to come and all the work that needed to be completed from the day before. He stares into the distance with all these thoughts going through his mind and as he gazes into the rearview mirror, looking at his own reflection he knows that the one thing he does not need to wonder is what the end of the day would look like. Ryan is certain that when his day is concluded and he must return home, what lay in wait regarding what Ryan called his marital situation was well defined.

It has been a long time since he felt the way he used to about getting home. Ryan questions himself, *is it the house? Is it the location of the house?* he pauses, knowing that he is not fooling himself, it is Amber. *I love her* Ryan thinks, as he stares at himself in the rearview mirror, his reflection looking back as if to reassure him or maybe to convince him. Ryan's deep thoughts are interrupted and his attention diverted to an out-of-focus scenario unfolding on the road ahead of him. It is the familiar lights of a police car and emergency vehicles that are illuminating the morning mist covering the landscape. It is the unmistakable sight of a vehicular accident that must have just happened as he can see the smoke still bellowing from under the hood as it lightly touches the morning sky.

Ryan slows as the other vehicles ahead of him slow. *Nosy people,* Ryan thinks. "People are always wanting to see something horrible," he says aloud. Of course as he passes the accident, he takes a look without giving any thought to being a nosy person himself. He thinks about it and laughs to himself. *Well the vehicle obviously left the road at some point,* Ryan thinks to himself, judging by the damage to the car and marks on the roadway, Ryan continues along and sees that vehicle at some point has taken out the 187-mile marker sign in the process. Ryan can see that the vehicle is almost unrecognizable, but it appears that whomever was in the vehicle had been extricated from the vehicle as they were now on a gurney being looked at by paramedics. The smell of the road flares fills the cab of the truck as Ryan passes, he can see the long blonde hair of what he thinks is a woman on the gurney but is unable able to get a clear view. Ryan sighs and thinks that is a horrible way to start the first day in December but hopes that the person is okay. As the lights fade behind him in the rear view mirror the blonde hair of the woman at the accident brings his thoughts back to Amber, not because of the blonde hair, Amber's hair was dirty brown, but the thought of what the husband or boyfriend of the woman in the accident if she had one would be going through right now.

Amber, whose maiden name was Dreyer, was a local girl with a bit of tomboy way to her. Amber was brought up in a single-parent (mother) family with little to no "supervision" so in some cases, she's a bit of a wild child. To her credit she has come a long way from the big hair days of the early 1980's, now a dirty brown replaces the bleach blonde hair of her youth. Ryan always thought that the dirty brown complimented her much better with her dark eyes, but he would have never said that aloud of course. Ambers mother, Barbara Chavez nèe Dreyer, was a lifelong resident in the area and whose family had been in Grantsville since the early fifties. Barbara was very proud of her German heritage and in a small way it was why she choose to introduce herself to everyone she meet as Barbara Chavez nèe Dreyer, always adding the Dreyer was German; however everyone just thought she liked the way it sounded. It was no secret to anyone in this small little town that Barbara was an alcoholic, not a fall down everyday kind of drunk but an alcoholic never the less. Amber's father Richard was also a lifelong resident and a bit of a drunk who had little family in the area. Many people did not know a lot about Richard or his family which consisted of his mother and brother. The local small talk was they simply wandered in to town one day. Richard was considered to be a Native American this due to his appearance and self-description, but many thought he was more Hispanic than anything. Richard was not what you would consider a model father and spent little "quality time" with Amber. It was rumored that when he did spend time with Amber he would leave her in the car sometimes for hours while he drank at the bar. Thankfully all of that was short lived for Amber as Richard committed suicide when she was ten years old; some in the town believed that is was in part the reason for her mother's struggle with alcohol.

In many ways Amber's childhood was a very tense and unpredictable situation; however despite those factors led a somewhat "normal life" but it was no secret that this contemptuous upbringing is what pushed her to Ryan and the need to get married at such a young age. Ryan was only twenty years of age at the time and Amber nineteen when they wed, not terribly young in a small town like Grantsville but still too young to really know what they were getting into. Ryan's parents were unremarkable by society standards. His mother, Mary, was a third-generation immigrant from Spain, a housewife by trade and although she only stood 4'11" she was a tough lady, she would tell you it was having gone through the Great Depression or having grown up poor was the source of her strength but in either case she was tough as nails. Ryan's father Charles was a second generation immigrant from Italy, who was considered to be handsome and very proud of whom he was; needless to say there was always a lot of food being made and, of course, lots of beer and wine in the house when Ryan was growing up. Ryan's mother was not much of a drinker which was of no consequence as his father always managed to pick up the slack and drank for breakfast, lunch and dinner. One question always came up regarding Ryan's father, if he was Italian how did he end up with the last name Allen and although the question came up from time to time his father never offered any explanation as to the discrepancy. It was rumored that Ryan's grandfather changed their last name in an attempt to maybe hide his past or to simply offer himself and his family better opportunities by having a Caucasian sounding last name but no one knew for sure. Ryan never gave it much thought although was grateful if the latter was true as it afforded him the opportunity to have a good job in a place where good jobs were few and far between. Today would be one of those days in which Ryan is grateful to have a good job, as he has spent the majority of this day doing paperwork and reading the newspaper. Ryan looks up at the clock as the minute hand strikes the top of the hour signifying the end of the work day, Ryan sighs as he gathers his things and heads out to his truck.

Another day has passed, and it has been a long one indeed. Ryan loses sight of the coal mine guard shack behind him in the rearview mirror, and the journey home begins. He has found that his anxiety grows exponentially as he arrives closer to home along with the familiar but unrecognizable guilt he feels. Thankfully the road from the mine where he has worked for the last several years is long and quiet, an important time to which he can assemble himself. Ryan smiles as "Hold On for One More Day" by Wilson Philips plays on the radio. The timing of the song is eerie, not to mention the fact that the song is a reminder of his father's death. This very song was playing when he passed away, a sort of last message from a man long gone now. He catches himself singing along with the radio twisting at his wedding ring around his finger, a nervous habit with no doubt hidden meaning. He steadies himself emotionally, looking in the rearview mirror as if allowing himself permission to greet her at the door without giving her a hint of what is behind his eyes. In the distance Ryan sees the spot where the accident occurred earlier that morning, he slows down and decides to stop. In one way Ryan thinks this is good, it will delay my arrival home as he laughs to himself, but something inside is telling him to take a look around. Ryan parks the truck off of the road and stands surveying the accident site. He can see the unmistakable tire marks and burnt patch on the road, and slowly walks along the eerie scene. As Ryan walks along a shimmering object on the ground catches his eye, he is not sure what it is but bends down to look at it. Ryan can see it is a necklace and picks it up, the chain is broken but the heart shaped pendant with a diamond at its center are still in good shape. Ryan looks at it for a moment and decides to take it with him and try to locate the owner. I am sure they would like this back he says to himself. Ryan stands on the road for a few more minutes as a strange feeling comes over him one he can't explain or in some ways doesn't even realize he is experiencing. Ryan walks back to the truck and gets in. He sits for a moment staring into the distance, he opens the ashtray and places the necklace inside and continues his journey home.

The sound and feel of the gravel road is unmistakable as it serves as confirmation that he is "Home." He parks in his usual spot but does not get out immediately. He sits for a moment, reassuring himself that he is prepared. He wants to make sure that she sees only the outside, always terrified that she may notice the slightest indications of what he feels inside. With a small exhale, he starts to get out of the truck. He reaches over and grabs his phone and lunch box. As the door opens, he can feel the enthusiasm of the wagging tale of Buddy, who is a German shepherd that he and Amber raised from a puppy. It was the same puppy that he and Amber discovered wandering the street several years earlier and decided to take him in. Buddy jumps around uncontrollably, he's happy to see his friend barking and panting as they approach the front door. As he pulls open the door, he can hear music playing ("Moon Over Georgia" by Shenandoah). It was Amber's thing to do when making dinner. Usually the genre was from the eighties, usually some big hair rock band but today a pleasant surprise as country music fills the air.

Amber leans out of the kitchen. "Hey, babe," she says.

Ryan just smiles at her and says, "I'm going to take a shower before dinner."

Amber with a mixing bowl in her hand softly says "Okay," turning around just enough to catch a glimpse of Ryan as he walks toward the bedroom. Amber stands there for a moment; her thoughts turn to a time that encompassed a much deeper greeting from Ryan when he returned home from work or from anywhere for that matter. She exhales and thinks how sad that is but knows that she feels powerless to change it. She knows that in reality what was before has since faded and this was as intimate a greeting as it was going to be for tonight.

Ryan steps into the shower and is soothed by the hot water streaming down his face. The comfort of the water is short-lived as he thinks, *How long can I go on pretending everything is okay? How long could I believe that she still assumes everything is normal, and how does she not know?* But then angrily thinks, *She rarely was concerned with anything and probably would not know what to say even if she suspected something.*

As the steam from the shower fills the bathroom Ryan continues to wonder in his mind, *What am I doing? How did I get here? ... Who am I?* He realizes that he is probably not alone, and these questions and others like them have haunted other men in similar situations since the beginning, the only difference is now these questions belong to him and have become a more familiar companion in the recent weeks. He finds himself becoming more and more concerned that these questions will never be answered, or that if he discovers the answers, he will regret the knowledge that he has gained. Ryan turns off the water and grabs a towel; he pauses to listen to the final drips from the shower head falling into the tub, a strangely comforting sound or more of a distraction to his thoughts. Either way signifying the end of any comfort the warm water afforded him.

As he dries the water from his face, the door opens slightly. Amber peeks in from the partially open door and smiles, "How was your day?" she asks.

Ryan, staring off into space and vigorously rubbing his head with the towel, says, "The normal stuff."

Amber pauses, looks down at the floor then at him, the awkward silence says more than either of them could express. She slowly turns away and closes the door, he looks in the mirror and takes a deep breath.

Ryan enters the kitchen. The table is set as usual; he pulls his chair and heavily sits, thinking of what he could talk about. It has to be something mindless, a pointless conversation, something that neither of them would even care about, but search as he might he can't find anything inside his mind that would be worth the effort. It is not that Amber would not listen or care, it is the thought that what if he says something that would bring to light what he has been feeling which of course would most certainly cause a fight or disagreement. Ryan is saddened because in the beginning of their relationship they agreed on everything and were able to tell each other anything. Ryan knows in his heart that the puppy love they once felt is gone and now all that remains is a stark contradiction on even the simplest of matters.

Dinner continues on with the usual uneventful small talk from Amber about the weather and Buddy's unwillingness to stop chasing his tail around the living room. As the end of dinner approaches Amber begins to pick up the dishes from the table. As she stands at the sink rinsing the dishes she asks, "Do you want to watch some TV?" Which of course was the normal activity every night so Ryan is not sure why it had to be a question every evening.

The journey to the couch is a long one and seems to be getting longer every day. As they sit together and watch mindless chatter Amber moves closer to Ryan and touches his hand gently. He knows what she means by it and knows that she only wants a show of affection from him; however he is struggling, battling with his feelings to return the gesture. He feels so guilty and angry at himself but at the same time can't help it, how could he have loved her so much and now has so much trouble expressing the simplest expressions of love?

As this normal and uneventful night draws to an end Amber is showing signs of fatigue and Ryan can see that she is falling asleep and as she begins to place her head on his shoulder, Ryan asks, "Are you ready for bed?" Amber nods yes, and begins to make her way to the bedroom.

As they enter the bedroom Ryan's sadness grows, this was once a place of fulfillment, he thinks, now empty after the long lonely journey from the couch. As he stares at the bed Ryan ponders to himself that the only journey that could possibly be any longer than the one from the living room, is the one from the door of the bedroom to the bed where he will soon lay with Amber. How can you think that he says to himself as he gets undressed, folding his clothes and placing them on the dresser. He watches with disdain as Amber undresses, leaving her clothes on the floor, adding to the pile of the clothes from the night before. They settle in under the sheets. Ryan places no effort to engage her; he strategically positions himself on the edge of the bed, making sure he will not accidentally rub against her. As he lies there he stares at the wall in the darkness, he can feel her moving, hoping that she will tire, and any plan for romance will quickly be abandoned.

As he feels himself drifting off to sleep, he prays that things will change and finds himself asking God for help, which is ironic because although raised in a Roman Catholic household, Ryan did not believe in God. Faith is something he wishes he had but knows it was a gift that he was unable or unworthy to receive. Amber on the other hand did have "faith" although you would never know it; it was more of a faith hinged upon the just-in-case-God-is-real theory more than anything else. I would imagine that it is what Christians would call a Lukewarm Christian. Amber would argue that her "faith" was one in which she could swear like a sailor and drink vodka to excess every night but "God" would understand and agree that as long as she asked for forgiveness she would be fine. Each time Amber would argue her view of religion, Ryan would think, *I wish I believed in her God, he sounds amazing.* But in the end, Ryan knows that he stands a better chance of the Egyptian god, Anubis, coming into his living room than the God she believes in being that good or real.

As the night wears on, Ryan is unable to sleep as he gazes at the clock. The seconds, minutes and hours slowly move along, Ryan is hopelessly mesmerized by the large green colored numbers of the clock glowing in the darkness. He mumbles to himself in frustration as he still cannot figure out a way to dim the light or how to take off the date from being displayed. Tonight he will have the privilege of staring at December 2nd, 3:33 a.m. with which Ryan thinks, *I don't need a reminder of what day it is. What does it matter, it is a day like any other day.* He rolls onto his back and stares at the ceiling, still tormented by the stupid green glow. Finally with his eyes heavy, he is able to slow his mind enough to fall asleep.

As he deepens in sleep, he is puzzled as to why if he is asleep he is still able to see the light of a small opening in the distance? He is puzzled and startled as he begins to feel a soft breeze on his skin and can hear what sounds like waves coming in from the ocean. He thinks to himself, *What a fabulous dream!* He can feel himself starting to move toward the light and sound, but he is not walking, it is like the feeling of standing on the escalator at the airport, which he once experienced while taking his first plane ride as a small boy when his parents took him to Disneyland. He knows this is a dream, of that he is sure! What he is not sure of is why he is going along with what is happening. *But it's a dream, right? What choice do I have?* He thinks as he giggles.

As the opening becomes wider, he can see what he thinks is an ocean, the white sands of its shores being slowly disrupted by the waves gently coming on to it. It is surreal as he sees the moonlight is shimmering off the water. Ryan finds himself thinking, *What a nice way to start a dream.* A stark contradiction to the life he faces when he awakens. He can now feel the sand under his feet, which he hates under normal circumstances; he has always worn shoes from the time he woke up until the time he went to bed. This was always a quirk which drove Amber crazy; she was always barefoot, so she would not be happy to see him enjoying this now. The breeze has now become a gentle comfort as his clothing sways with its touch. Ryan adjusts his eyes, trying to make sense of what he is seeing. Along the edge of the water in the distance, he can see a figure, it is the unmistakable figure of a woman. Her curvy silhouette and the distinct outline of her symmetry is breathtaking. He is not sure why but he keeps moving closer, thankful for the force propelling him.

As the figure becomes more and more visible, the silhouette becomes a vision of beauty that causes him to pause in breath; she is what you would envision, if you pictured a beautiful woman. Her long blonde hair and crystal blue eyes only added to the amazing body before him. He looks away a feeling of guilt, shame and the feeling of doing something wrong fills him as the ghostly image takes form and looks into his eyes. His heart beat increases. He can feel the pulse in his neck like the sound of a tap dancer on a hard wood floor, but he is not sure why this dream feels more real than any other he has had in his life. He questions himself and, of course, his own mental stability as to how this dream is managing to maintain its form, no fuzziness, no sudden jerks from one image to the next. The questions are building up in his head faster than he can understand what those questions are. The answers, if they are coming are not so quick to make themselves immediately apparent.

Before he can make sense of the moment, the mysterious woman speaks. "Hi," the young woman whispers slowly, cautiously looking up at Ryan with her crystal blues eyes, her long eyelashes batting with a seductive yet innocent rhythm.

Ryan struggles to respond; he knows the words but is unable to make them come out. In his head, the word "hi," which he is sure he has vocalized several million times in his life, now refuses to make its way through his lips. The young woman with a smile and a slight giggle says, "I'm Sara."

Ryan continues to struggle but manages to mutter, "H-Hi. I mean hello. I'm Ryan."

"It is a pleasure to meet you, Ryan."

Ryan gazes and says, "You look so real."

"Why shouldn't I?"

"Because this is a dream?" Ryan whispers.

"Why, because you had to be asleep to get here?"

"That is what a dream is,"

Sara reaches out and touching Ryan's arm whispers, "There is so much I have to show you."

Ryan struggles to understand what is happening and why he can feel the touch of her hand, not only on his arm but in his heart. As he gazes at Sara struggling to find the right words, his eyes move to an object around her neck, it is a necklace with a heart shaped pendant and a diamond at its center. In Ryan's mind he is not sure why but he cannot take his eyes off of it.

"What are you looking at?" Sara says giggling.

"No…no I was looking at your necklace. It's beautiful."

Sara places her hand over it in adornment, "Thank you, I never take it off." she says, "It was a gift from my mother."

"Who are you?" Ryan asks.

"Who are you?" Sara quickly replies, Ryan looks down at the sand then over the water, unsure of what to say next. Sara tilts Ryan's head up with her finger "Would you like to walk with me?" Sara asks.

Ryan, without giving any response, begins to walk alongside her, as she begins to walk. As they stroll along, the unwavering feeling of this can't be real pesters Ryan. *This is not real!* Ryan keeps repeating to himself over and over again but without hesitation continues on as Sara explains, "I have been coming to this same beach every day, but

I have never met anyone else here before and certainly not anyone like you," as she squeezes his hand. Sara goes on to say that although she is not certain why she comes to this same beach every day, somehow she is drawn to it.

Ryan, not sure what to say, asks Sara, "Where do you live—where do you work?" As he asks these questions, the feeling of "Am I going insane?" crosses his mind. *I am asking a dream where it lives and works.* Ryan questions his own sanity and as he does, Sara abruptly stops walking, turns to Ryan, and says, "You have a nice smile."

Ryan is flattered by Sara's off handed comment but is not sure how to respond so instead he simply smiles as Sara turns and continues to walk. As they walk along the beach, Ryan begins to fill with dread, knowing that it will not be long before he wakes up. Ryan does not want to let on to Sara that he is filling up with fear inside and knows that soon this wonderful journey will be coming to an end. Ryan turns to Sara and says, "I know this is a dream and I know that sooner or later it will be over, but I want you to know that I wish I could stay longer."

Sara grasps his hand, "Don't worry. *Love always finds a way.*"

Ryan thinks nothing of her comment and hastily says, "I'll see you when I come back?" At that moment thinking that this is a dream, how would he come back if it is a dream and what is she talking about love will find a way?

Sara looks out at the ocean, a strange calm in her voice, "I have made my way here every day since I have been here, I don't know why nor do I care to understand it. All I know is that I am here now and in doing that I have found you and you have found me. So if both of us are here, someone or something wants us here."

Ryan, with a puzzled look on his face asks, "Found our way where?—Someone who?"

Sara smiles and says, "If you figure that out, maybe you will have figured it out for the both of us!"

Ryan begins to feel the weight of the blankets on his skin, the familiar smell of the bedroom begins to fill his nostrils. The grip of Sara's hand begins to loosen, and she begins to fade. Sara smiles one last time and looks away.

Ryan gasps and sits up in bed, the blankets thrown off both him and Amber, he is shaken and frantically looks around the room as he tries to make sense of what has happened.

Amber is awakened by the sudden jolt, she touches Ryan's arm and whispers, "Are you okay?"

"I'm fine." Ryan says as he breaths heavily and moves to the end of the bed, still unable to make sense of what happened and what he is feeling. *This makes no sense. Why do I remember the entire dream? I never remember what I dream about he thinks* as he stares at the floor and shakes his head. Buddy moves toward him, wagging his tail and whimpering. He pats Buddy on the head and neck, rubbing his coat. Buddy looks up at him, it is almost like he feels or senses something is not right, it's as if he is afraid. "You are a good boy," Ryan says, "let's go get you something to eat."

In his mind, Ryan is thinking it's just a dream; he shakes his head and quietly says, "How foolish. Of course, it was a dream." Ryan makes his way to the bathroom then into the kitchen to get Buddy a snack, and despite the evenings events it is time to start another day, but what Ryan did not know at that moment is how this day would be different. A small smile comes over his face as he thinks of the dream he had and the beautiful girl he met, "Sara," he says to himself. Secretly, he is hoping that he will be able to keep her memory fresh in his mind but at the same time he is ashamed that he might. *Why would you keep the memory of a dream*, he thinks, *when I have a reality here with Amber.* Although he has a sense that this is wrong, the feeling he felt on that beach is a missing feeling that has been absent from his reality for a long time.

As he readies himself to leave for work, Amber follows him out the front door and gives him a hug, which she has done hundreds of times before; however, this one was different. He panics a little thinking that she knows, then he thinks to himself, *You are really losing it, how could she possibly know?*

As Ryan drives away from home, he looks back in the rearview mirror at Amber who is still standing at the front door and at Buddy who is still sitting on the porch, staring at the truck as it pulls away. Ryan ponders as he looks away from the mirror, *strange, right? She has never done that before.*

As Ryan is driving he thinks about Amber and her unusual gesture of coming out on the porch, then about Buddy and his strange attentiveness, but most of all thinks of Sara and the hope to have the same dream again someday, another dream that will allow him to see her again. Ryan cracks open the window and lights a cigarette, he thinks *do you know how insane that sounds.* He smiles and laughs at himself. "You are crazy," he says laughing to himself. "You are crazy."

CHAPTER
TWO

The road to the coal mine is a long one, it is a forty-five minute drive one way. It would appear that coal is not one of those minerals that has a choice on whether or not it is convenient to get to it, or where you can find it, for that matter, but Ryan is thankful for it as it has allowed him to have a good job in a land with few jobs. The Canyon Coal Mining Company was not a locally owned company which was a problem for some of the locals, but it did offer higher than normal pay and benefits, which elevated some of that friction. In this part of the world if you would like to work it is either the paper mill or the prison, which neither of these two jobs would be something you would choose to do, so Ryan makes this long trip over and over again. This is not, of course, the life that he envisioned for himself, but it is the life he has nevertheless.

Ryan was a bit of a dreamer. As a teenager, he wanted to be an actor, an artist or maybe a musician, but of course his father was a miner as were his two brothers, sister, and brother-in-law. So according to his father this meaningless pursuit of something that could not possibly make any money, or provide for a family was simply out of the question and was not an option in his father's eyes. Ryan remembers his father telling him whenever he wanted to draw or paint hoping to make it a career. "What are you going to do, draw pictures all your life?" So, of course, he followed in his father's footsteps.

During his father's time, uranium was the mineral of choice, but the boom was over and now it was coal. Ryan was able to get on with the Canyon Coal Mining Company not as a product of his high marks in high school but instead the way everyone in a small town gets a job, a favor from a friend or family member. Ryan was sort of an exception to the rule when it came to following in your father's footsteps as he was a mechanic by trade, a skill he learned so not really a "Miner". Ryan's family was well regarded in the community, so he would fall under the family member who knows someone who owes them a favor rule, thus the reason he is not a miner and got a job at a mine. The familiar silhouette of the gatehouse appears in the distance.

As Ryan pulls up, Mark Gottie is there to greet him; Mark who was, of course, a local and a bit of a drunk was someone who could not find work in town, but managed to land the job of security guard for the mine. Which as it turns out was a job he loved as he got paid to do almost nothing and afforded him the ability to talk to all the people he knew at the same time. Mark whose shirt was always stained with coffee and seemed to be two sizes too small for him, gives Ryan the same old greeting as he enters, a halfhearted salute, Ryan laughs every time and waves back being polite which is a curse of living in a small town.

As he approaches the shop, it is the usual cast of characters there to greet him. Fred Dryer is a fellow mechanic, a nice guy who had a reputation with the ladies. He had been married five times, one of which he married and divorced twice to the same woman and had a few kids with each of them. Frank Stanton, who was a supervisor for the mill and who oversees the mechanic shop, stands there wearing a tie. He always wore a tie, which makes no sense in a mine, but it would seem he just liked ties. Frank was the son of a superintendent of the mine and got the job because of it. Everyone who knew him felt he would not be the person anyone would have selected for that job, but he was a nice guy which kind of made up for the fact that he was not the smartest person you would ever meet. And, of course, last but not least, Charlie Dennis; who has been around the mine since its inception. No one ever really knows what his official title or job is, he just sorts of hangs around the mine, doing odd jobs and telling jokes.

The day begins as any other with a short time spent on paperwork that no one ever looked at then a quick cup of coffee before heading out onto the shop floor. Ryan spends part of this time thinking about the dream he had, the name Sara is like a soft voice in his head he can hear in the distance. I wonder if that is how people with schizophrenia start hearing voices he thinks and laughs to himself.

As he sits there daydreaming, still trying to make sense of it, Charlie touches him on the shoulder startling Ryan and asks "What the heck are you doing, sleeping?" as he laughs.

Ryan flinches, "Dammit Charlie you scared me!" Charlie continues to laugh, "Charlie, leave me the hell alone!" Ryan shouts as Charlie continues to laugh as he leaves the small area where Ryan had situated himself.

Ryan finishes up his paperwork, grabs his hard hat and gloves, and heads out to the shop floor. The day would go on as normal until his cell phone rings. Ryan looks up at the clock and sees it is 10:00

a.m., a typical time that Amber would call to make small talk. He looks down at the screen and sees that he is correct, it is her. He takes a deep breath and answers, "Hey, babe."

"How are you?"

"Same old stuff." He says, "How is your day?"

"Fine." Amber replies.

Ryan pins the phone against his cheek and shoulder and continues working, not necessarily paying attention to what Amber is saying but still listening; this, of course, is not because he is mean or rude but because it was the normal daily routine that has played out time and time again. As they talk, Ryan is unaware that this conversation would not be so similar.

Amber pauses, "I was thinking of coming to see you for lunch today?"

Ryan takes the phone away from his ear and looks at the phone screen, then places it back against his ear, "Lunch…Here?" Ryan replies "Is everything okay?"

"Yes, everything is fine" Amber says, "I just wanted to see you and talk to you."

Ryan's mind begins to race. "I really don't think that is a good idea."

Amber quickly interrupts, "It's important."

Ryan's hands begin to sweat, and the voice in his head is arguing against it, but reluctantly he agrees, "Okay, I'll see you in a while then."

"Okay, love you." Amber says.

"Love you too."

Ryan hangs up the phone, stares at it for a moment and goes back to what he was doing, thinking, *What now?*

As Ryan continues to go on with his work the day now slows to a crawl, the feeling is like that of someone on death row awaiting execution as he continues anticipating Amber's arrival. It is now the afternoon, and his cell phone rings, Ryan takes a deep breath and looks toward the clock on the wall which is showing twelve. *Time is up*, he thinks. He takes another deep breath and opens the screen. "Hi, babe, are you here?"

"Yes, I am at the gate."

"I'll be right there," Ryan replies and begins to walk down to the gate. As he is walking he passes Charlie on the way.

"Wife day huh, Ryan?" Charlie shouts.

Ryan says nothing, nods, and waves him off. He sees that Amber is standing outside the car as he walks toward her, he waves, Amber waves back and smiles. Ryan opens the passenger door for Amber then walks around the car to the driver's side and gets into the car. Ryan starts the car and pulls off farther to the side of the road just south of the gatehouse so not to block the main entrance to the mill.

"So what's up, babe…what's wrong?" Ryan asks with a slight hesitation.

"I wanted to talk to you about how things have been going lately…between you and I."

Ryan stares down at the floor. "Like what?" Ryan replies, thinking, *She has noticed the change.*

"I want us to be happy again.—I want us to laugh and we just don't do that anymore."

"I know, but what would you like me to do?"

"I want you to try." Amber says.

"Try what?" Ryan says in a frustrated tone.

Amber sits forward and in a raised tone says, "I did not come out here to fight with you. I came out here to tell you that I think we need to start thinking about trying again for a baby."

"How does that help?"

What they both know is that several years earlier, Amber had become pregnant but did not carry to term. Ryan believed that this miscarriage was in part the reason for the distance between them now. However, if you were to ask Amber, she would say that it was the resentment toward her from Ryan that began the split. All of this was like a small splinter that wedged itself in a finger, it is not so painful that it is unbearable yet not so minor that it could be forgotten.

"I don't think we should talk about this right now." Ryan says.

"Then when?"

"I have to go."

Amber looks down at the floor as the tears begin to build and nods, saying, "I'll see you at home."

Ryan says, "Okay, love you." Amber looks away as the door opens. Ryan leans in the open door and says, "We will talk about this later."

"Of course we will," Amber says with a look of doubt and disgust on her face.

Ryan watches as Amber drives away, thinking, *I wish I was on a beach right now.* With the thought of the peace he felt with Sara ever so softly in those thoughts.

Despite the drama of the afternoon, the day progresses as usual after such an unusual event, but Ryan knows that soon he will have to continue the conversation that he successfully ended earlier in the day. As the clock winds down, the sunset begins to signal the end of day. Ryan understands that as far as this day goes, he has delayed the inevitable as long as he can. He knows that the long ride home is not going to last as long as he would hope.

As he drives along, a thought appears in his mind, *Sara...* He shakes his head and tries to focus on the conversation he will have with Amber. He thinks of what he wants to say, what he will say, and of course, what she will surely say when that time comes. He continues to go over the night's event in his mind which will soon unfold but cannot keep from glancing with his mind's eye to Sara looking back at him. As he pulls into the driveway, he sees that Buddy is already waiting on the porch, almost as if he had been there for some time staring down the road, awaiting his arrival. The jumping and panting begin immediately as Ryan exits his truck. Ryan pats Buddy as he walks alongside him into the house. "Hey Buddy... Good boy."

As he enters the house, Amber is not in the kitchen tonight. As the door opens, he sees Amber sitting on the couch with a glass of wine in her hand. There will be no escape to the shower tonight, and it appears no dinner. Ryan places his things on the edge of the coffee table and sits down. The feeling of distance between them is overwhelming, and the silence is deafening.

"Do you love me?" Amber asks.

"Of course I love you."

"Do you hate me for losing the baby?"

"No, I don't hate you." Ryan says. "Why would you say that?"

"Then why can't we try?"

"It's complicated."

"What is so complicated about wanting to have a family… What is so complicated about wanting to have a family with you?"

Ryan sighs and looks away.

"Ryan, look at me."… "Ryan look at me." she says in a louder tone.

"What do you want me to say, Amber!" Ryan shouts, his frustration and anger feels like heat being applied to the back of his neck and it is uncomfortable. He fidgets, as the tingling on his skin caused by the anxiety is becoming irritating.

"I want you to say we can try." Amber says with the tears now building in her eyes but somehow manage to stay in her eyes.

Ryan oddly thinks that those are a lot of tears to just stay there, and then thinks what you are thinking about? Ryan looks at Amber and, in an effort to just end all this, says, "Okay, we can try."

Amber pauses, "Do you mean it?"

Ryan pauses, his inner voices screaming to tell her the truth which is that he does not want to try, that he is not sure about their relationship and a thousand other responses to which he replies, "Yes, I mean it."

Amber places her glass of wine on the coffee table and reaches for Ryan, kissing him on the lips as her tears transfer onto his face. Without thought, Amber's breathing has become passionate, the kissing becomes more than an end to the argument, her breathing has become heavier with the sound of arousal. Ryan reaches his hand around her waist and pulls her close; he still wants her sexually despite what he feels emotionally. Amber begins to remove his shirt as she pulls at her own. The weight of their embrace forces them onto the couch. Ryan begins to remove her bra and her milky white breasts are now pressing against him. He feels the erotic nature of what is happening, and for a moment almost feels normal, provided the unusual way all of this started. Ryan hastily removes her pants and as he tries to remove them her panties get tangled together with her pants and merge as they slide down her thighs. In touching her softly, Amber quivers in excitement.

Ryan moves Amber beneath him and penetrates her, the softness of her accepting the hardness of his body. Amber arches and lets out a gasp as their bodies become one. Ryan lifts off of Amber slightly and looks down at Amber her hair is partially covering her face. He gently moves her hair to see her face and as her face is revealed, Ryan abruptly stops and gazes at the face of the woman beneath him. It is not Amber's face he is looking at but it is Sara. His momentum inside Amber slows Ryan shakes his head and rapidly closes and opens his eyes as if this could somehow correct his vision, but as he looks again it is not Amber…it is the girl he met in his dream.

"What's wrong?" Amber says.

Ryan shakes his head and looks again, Sara's face is gone and he can now see it is Amber.

Amber, startled arches up and looks at Ryan. "What is it?"

Ryan, still breathing heavily, says, "Nothing, it's nothing."

Amber, unsure of what to do, pulls away, and her eyes fill with tears. She looks at Ryan and gets up from the couch she quietly gathers her clothes and walks to the bedroom, closing the door behind her. Ryan sits on the couch, and as the silence begins to fill the room, he is afraid, not of the silence and not of what just happened with Amber but the fear of feeling a moment of happiness when seeing Sara's face. Ryan makes no effort to go to the bedroom, the couch will be his refuge tonight, and besides what would he say? What could he say? Ryan is now faced with the thought that a delusion, this dream is now affecting and complicating an already difficult situation, but how can he remedy a dream or a vision? Especially one that has given him a moment of happiness of which he is unable to get from his physical wife.

Maybe I need help, this is all in my mind and I need help. As he sits in the darkness, he ponders, *Who would I tell, what could I tell? And what would happen once I did?* The thought that a crazy dream could cause all this is unfathomable. The feelings he was experiencing over what could not possibly be real is sheer insanity, he thinks. The night would be a long one as Ryan struggles to sleep, the sadness of the situation still lingering as he drifts off to sleep.

Ryan is suddenly awakened by a gentle touch; he is startled and for a moment thinks, *Amber,* as he slowly opens his eyes, expecting a continuation of the nights events. As the image comes into view he exhales in relief as he sees that it is Sara. "What are you doing here?" Ryan asks with utter disbelief in his voice.

"Looking for you." Sara replies, smiling.

Ryan looks around, and the living room, the couch is gone, and he is now lying next to a downed palm tree. In the living room, he thinks, *Wake up*, he says to himself, *Wake up*. It is then he realizes he is awake and back on the beach; he takes a second and third look and cannot bring himself to believe it is real.

"This is not real." Ryan whispers.

"Why, because you are dreaming?" Sara replies.

"Yes!"

"So do you want me to leave?"

Ryan pauses and says, "No…I don't want you to leave…no."

"Okay." Sara replies as she embraces Ryan.

Ryan returns the embrace holding her firmly as his eyes scour the beach with wonder and disbelief. Ryan asks, "Do you know why this is happening…Do you know how this is happening?"

"No, I don't know why…I don't know how. All I know is that I don't want to leave."

"Were you a real person?" Ryan asks.

"What is real?"—"You are here, are you a real person?" Sara says, "What would it matter if I was or wasn't a real person?"

"I know." Ryan says. "I know, but where is here?—How is it this all feels so real and why?"

Sara playfully stops him, "What does it matter? We are here now. Are we going to waste it trying to figure this all out?"

"I guess not." Ryan says.

The next several hours go by as quickly as they came, and the overwhelming feeling of connection is more real than he can even understand, and even though Ryan knows that this is not any reality he has ever been a part, he does not want to leave it. As the night wears on, Sara tells of the things that she has seen, remembers and of who or what she was. Ryan is beginning to see that this is more than a dream. He could not possibly be creating all this in his mind, and this has to be coming from somewhere he ponders, and there must be a reason, Why him? …Why her? *Obviously, this is something more than a dream,* Ryan thinks, *but how? Why?* Sara begins to explain that she does not know how long she has been here, wherever here is, but does know that her journey began as a small opening of light in her mind's eye, the same type of opening that Ryan saw the first time he and Sara met. *This cannot be a coincidence*, Ryan thinks to himself, *there must be something to this.* In an awkward moment and without warning Sara leans toward Ryan kissing him on the lips, Ryan pulls away just for a second then leans in and passionately kisses Sara. Suddenly Sara pulls away. Ryan begins to feel a warm sensation on his cheek, and the warmth seems to be growing in intensity. He realizes what's happening. *I'm waking up*, he thinks. He hurriedly tells Sara "I will be back, Sara…I will be back." as she fades into the darkness.

The sunlight coming through the kitchen window has made its way onto his face. The sun, of course, has brought the morning and along with it the sadness of being back and the shame of wanting to return to the beach with Sara. Ryan hears Amber moving around the bedroom, and he is unsure of what he would or should say. He slowly makes the move to the bedroom and gently knocks on the door.

"Amber?" he says softly. He opens the door slightly; he can see Amber's reflection in the mirror putting on her makeup. Without saying anything he comes up behind and hugs her. "Good morning." Ryan whispers.

Amber says nothing in return. As they embrace, Ryan looks toward the couch where he spent the night. The image of Sara is clearly in this thoughts. A sense of guilt comes over him for what happened, but it was a dream, right? That is not really cheating. He struggles to reconcile what happened in his mind yet hopes that it will happen again. Ryan goes over all that has happened in his mind. This feeling or whatever it was for Sara is too strong for it to be what amounts to a dream. In his mind, he's certain of what he felt. *But do*

I still need to know? If I only knew what it was? But I don't even know what I am looking for, Ryan thinks.

Amber presses her body back against Ryan while placing her hands on his arms which are wrapped around her. *What about Amber?* he thinks, *the woman I have loved for so long. Amber is real, she is a physical person. I am losing my mind.*

Amber pulls away slightly "I need to get going on my day" she says as she lets him go and kisses him on the cheek. He watches her as she goes into the bedroom, saddened for what she is going through yet unable to offer any comfort. Ryan gathers his thoughts and prepares for the day. As he finishes getting ready, he tells himself that it is time to face a very real reality. The reality that the world he has seen can't possibly exist and the woman he wants is someone who isn't real. *How can I undo this?* He thinks, *How?*

CHAPTER
THREE

Another day has passed, Ryan awakens from a sleepless and restless night, the dream from the night before is still vivid in his mind and he is now tormented by the thought of what might be on the horizon. Ryan drives along, struggling to make sense of all that has happened. His hands are shaky, and a slight pressure begins to build behind his eyes. He squints and applies pressure with his hand to the back of his neck, his mind racing.

The faint and distant image of the mill gate begins to slowly appear on the horizon. Mark, with a cup of coffee in his hand and a cigarette in the other, waves at Ryan as he enters the gate. Ryan nods and offers a small wave as a kind gesture in a not so good morning. Ryan parks his truck but in doing so forgets to put it in park; as he turns off the engine and gets out, suddenly he feels the truck roll forward as he opens the door. Ryan quickly grabs for the shift knob and forces the truck into gear. Still startled he glances at the side mirror, and he sees that the man staring back at him is someone he doesn't recognize, a man without answers, tired and lost.

Ryan still shaky from the morning's events fumbles with his keys and lunch box, as he makes his way to the office. He is desperately trying to avoid any contact with anyone who could see him in this disheveled state. Ryan reaches his small work area and sits down, his hand rests on the desk as he gathers his thoughts and takes a breath. He can feel his sweaty palms on the desktop as he gathers himself as best he can and shuffles through the paperwork. As he tries to settle in for the day he wants nothing more than to turn this morning around.

As the morning moves along, things appear to take on a lighter feel and he has even stopped shaking. Charlie who has always managed to make any moment light has made an appearance where Ryan is and has placed a small grin on Ryan's face.

Charlie says to Ryan, who has turned around in his chair and is now facing Charlie, "Did I ever tell you about when Bubba and his brother went to truck driving school?"

Ryan knew what was coming next. Charlie was the type of person who told the same jokes over and over again and told them as if it was the first time he ever told you. But today it was a welcome and well needed break that Ryan could use. Ryan shakes his head as to say, "No, I did not hear that one."

"So Bubba and his brother are in a CDL class, and the instructor asks Bubba, "Bubba, you are in a flat wagon with twenty tons of steel, headed down a 45-grade, and your brakes go out, and at the bottom of the hill, there is a broken-down school bus full of children in your lane. What do you do?'"

Ryan grins.

"Bubba looks at the instructor and says, "I am going to wake up Bud, who is the brother." Charlie adds. The instructor looks at Bubba and says, "Bubba! You are on a 45-grade, no brakes, hauling twenty tons of steel, and you are on a collision path with a bus full of children. What do you do?" "I am going to wake up Bud." Bubba answers. The instructor looks at Bubba with confusion and anger and says, "Why in the hell would you wake up Bud?' Charlie begins to laugh before he has even completed the joke and says, "Because Bud ain't ever seen a wreck like the one he is about to see!" with which Charlie begins to laugh uncontrollably and as always looks to the person he is telling the joke, too, expecting them to share the same response.

Ryan bends over laughing in exaggeration, "That is a good one…That is a good one."

Charlie continues to laugh as he walks away, muttering, "I'm going to wake up Bud."

Ryan looks on as Charlie leaves the area and is thankful knowing that watching and listening to Charlie tell his joke has offered a small but much needed moment of levity to what is actually happening around him. Ryan sits for a moment and decides to get going on with actual work. He completes his paperwork, grabs his hard hat and gloves, and heads out onto the shop floor.

As Ryan makes his way onto the shop floor, Frank makes eye contact and shouts out, "We need to get on the brakes for the DAC." (The DAC is a DAC 120 DE haul truck which hauls 120 short tons and was built between 1988 and 1990).

Ryan just waves and silently says to himself, "I know, you idiot."

Ryan gathers his tools and makes his way to the DAC, as he looks up at the massive piece of equipment and sighs. Ryan can hear Frank's voice in the background shouting to him that the fuel truck sitting in the bay was brought in, but no one said what is wrong with it. Ryan dismisses Frank, crawls under the DAC and begins to work, as it turns out the only person who heard anything regarding the fuel truck that morning was Fred who himself was not sure what was wrong with it, but did hear it almost caused an accident. As it turn out the fuel truck had been brought in that night because the accelerator had been sticking, which almost caused the accident out on the dragline. The foreman from the night crew wanted it to be checked out and repaired before it was moved or returned to service, but that information was never passed along to the day crew. Ryan can hear the usual commotion in the background, but somewhere inside of him, something is telling him that something is not right. It is a feeling of something almost mystical has filled the air, as if it were vapor or smoke. Ryan pauses but for now ignores the feeling, thinking that it is nothing more than his mind, that of course along with all he had been through in the last several days. Ryan is trying but cannot shake the feeling; he knows that this is something more than that. Ryan steps out from under the DAC to take a look around.

Ryan turns his attention to the sound of Fred's voice, who he can hear yelling but does not see immediately. He recognizes that Fred was yelling towards Charlie, Fred is yelling as loud as he can but it appears Charlie is unable to hear him over the noise of the shop and is not responding. Ryan locates Fred and watches him as he hurriedly walks toward the fuel truck screaming, "Charlie…hang on that fuel truck has a problem…Charlie…Charlie!" Suddenly everything slows down as if Ryan is watching a scene from *The Matrix* movie. Ryan's eyes move to where Charlie is, he sees Charlie getting into the fuel truck which is facing directly toward where he is working and hears it start; Ryan's eyes move back to Fred who is now waving his arms frantically, yelling, "C h a r l i e………C h a r l i e!" trying to get Charlie's attention. Ryan stares for a moment as everything becomes strangely vivid and all the sounds of the shop have blended together. Ryan knows that he should do something but for some unknown reason, he continues to stare. His attention turns back to Charlie and the fuel truck, his arm hanging onto the door frame which he left open slightly. Ryan takes a deep breath, his focus now on the truck lurching toward him. Ryan can see Charlie's face which is obviously puzzled and scared; he can also see as Charlie tugs at the steering wheel and attempts to close the door to the truck. Ryan takes a deep breath, his focus now on the truck lurching toward him.

Ryan can hear Charlie is screaming "Whoa! Whoa!" and can see that he is frantically trying to figure out what to do. Ryan is paralyzed; he can see the truck heading straight toward him. As it approaches, he wants to get out of the way but is unable to move. The slowing of time continues, and what has taken seconds now seems like minutes or hours. The sound of Charlie's screams echo through the shop, like some sort of movie sound track added into this moment to add a hint of drama to an already dramatic situation. Ryan stands there as the fuel truck appears to be moving as if it is casually strolling through the park, and as suddenly as it had begun, the horrible reality hits. The fuel truck smashes into the side of the DAC, pinning Ryan between the fuel truck and the enormous tire of the DAC.

The sound of the impact is deafening, like the sound of nails on a chalkboard while at the same time pots and pans were being slammed together all at once. As the sound continues, it is quickly substituted with the smell of diesel fuel. Ryan shakes his head, trying to stop the ringing in his ears. He can feel the warm, smooth trickle of blood as it migrates down his face. *I'm alive!* Ryan thinks. He is perplexed as to why he can understand his situation but can feel no pain, and is unable to move. Strangely Ryan can feel the tread of the tire on his back, and thinks I am obviously being pressed against it. Ryan's focus moves to the pressure of the metal resting upon his chest and legs that is forcing him into the tire; it is suffocating, and he is having trouble catching his breath. He can hear the screams of the people in the shop who are all now running toward him and deciding what to do. The scene is chaotic, and all Ryan can think of is *Why isn't anyone moving the truck?*

Ryan can hear Frank who is shouting, "Don't move!—Ryan don't move!"

Ryan thinks, *He is so stupid. I can't move,* and then the sudden rush of adrenaline caused by the shock passes and Ryan begins to have a small indication of pain all over his body, which is increasing to a very distinct discomfort. The sound of people screaming and other unexplained noises fill the air. The smell of burnt rubber, smoke, and diesel fuel fill Ryan's senses with every breath. It seems like an eternity, which is fitting to accommodate the many thoughts that are racing through his mind. He is surprised that in this moment of trauma, pain, and confusion, his thoughts focus on the face of Sara, then thinks what about Amber? As these thoughts go through his mind it feels like he has been pinned for an eternity seemingly with no one helping or even trying to get help, but then in the distance Ryan can hear the sirens of the rescue vehicles as they approach.

Ryan is jolted into reality as the first responders begin to talk to him, asking him, "Where does it hurt?…Try not to move." As he looks through the arms and hands of his rescuers, he can see Charlie crouched down on the floor a short distance away crippled with guilt. Ryan remembers feeling bad for Charlie and even in that moment, wanting to say to him that it is okay, *"I am okay."*

The amount of people around him is claustrophobic, and although he knows that they are there to help, he wants them to go away. The rush of pain brings him back to the moment as the fuel truck is slowly moved away. He can partially see there is a reddish liquid on the floor and thinks that it's a lot of oil. Where is all the oil coming from? Then a voice somewhere inside taps him on the shoulder, telling him that's not oil, it's blood, your blood. He grimaces as he is laid out flat on the cold concrete. The rescue workers are doing their best to comfort Ryan, while at the same time the look on their faces is not one of confidence. The pressure from his rescuer's hands is pronounced and on several places over his body. *This cannot be good.* He thinks and feels helpless as he is rolled onto his side and a backboard is slid underneath him. The tightness of the stabilizing collar placed on his neck is causing panic. *This is not a good time to be claustrophobic*, he thinks.

Suddenly he feels himself abruptly lifted off of the floor, the sound of small wheels running along the concrete is faint in the distance as he is moved to the ambulance. As he is loaded into the ambulance, he stares at the celling of the ambulance which he marks off the list of things he never thought he would see and as the ambulance races away he thinks, *I've never been inside an ambulance before either.* Odd thoughts for someone who was involved in a horrific accident just moments before. His thoughts quickly change as the pain now is unbearable, and his ability to remain awake is fading. Ryan can hear the sounds of the paramedics calling in his diagnosis to the hospital that is awaiting him. "Zuni Memorial Hospital, this is Unit 355... *Go ahead Unit 355...* We have a thirty-nine-year-old male, massive head injuries and trauma to the torso due to a work site accident, twenty-five minute extraction, patient is semi-conscious, has a 20 cm cut to the right side of his head and several contusions and abrasions to his face and the back of his head. Patient appears to have a compound fracture of his left humeral, a puncture on the right side just below his right pectoral muscle. HR 105, BP 160/90, RR 16. Splinted, immobilized, IV x2, Morphine 2mg, ETA thirty minutes....Copy unit 355, thirty minutes."

Ryan can hear the other paramedic attending to him keep repeating, "Ryan, stay with us, try to stay awake." Ryan stares up at the white ceiling, he can hear his heartbeat like a distant Indian drum as his shallow breathing muffles the sound. Suddenly everything fades to black is as if a hood was placed over his head. He cannot understand what is happening but he is now looking down at himself; he watches as his body violently spasms, the feeling he remembers as a child when he tried to put a paper clip in the electrical wall socket of his childhood home. A flash of what he thinks is Sara's face appears then fades as the force of the defibrillation machine used by the paramedics shocks him back to life.

Ryan is violently thrusted back into his body, and he hears, "We have a pulse—We have a pulse."

All at once the ambulance comes to a stop; the jerking of the gurney moves back and forth as the paramedics remove him from the ambulance and roll him into the emergency room. The lights of the ceiling are becoming less bright as the gurney moves along the long corridor. He wants to close his eyes just for a moment, but the paramedic from the ambulance is relentless in his request to stay awake. The sound of the gurney hitting the swinging doors of the examination room is dramatic and Ryan can hear the doctors and nurses talking and rushing around him. Ryan feels the weight of his body moving from the gurney to the bed as he hears "Okay, one...

two…three. Let's start a line and we are going to need a vascular surgeon on this one."

As the Emergency Room Physician and staff move around, he can hear someone talking to him. "Mr. Allen, I am Dr. Michaels, can you hear me? Can you tell me where it hurts, Mr. Allen?"

Ryan just stares up at the ceiling, a sense of calm has come over him like a warm blanket. He realizes that he has not thought of Amber or if anyone called her to let her know what has happened. Oddly, instead he thinks of Sara and the time he spent with her on the beach. A tear cascades across his cheek, not for his situation he now finds himself in nor for Amber but for Sara. *How will she know what happened to me?* he thinks as another tear cascades. He thinks of how Sara would be left to wonder when he never comes back.

A loud screeching voice engulfs the room. "His wife is here!" a nurse cries out.

"Keep her out, once we stabilize him, she can have a moment!" The doctor shouts.

Ryan tries to look around; his eyes search the room frantically but he is unable to turn his head, restricted by the neck brace that the paramedics placed on him. The uncomfortable pressure caused by the neck brace on his head and neck is claustrophobic as he is on the onset of a full panic attack as he squirms looking for Amber. Ryan can't see Amber, he wants to at the very least see something familiar should he not make it out of the room. To at least tell her that he was sorry and that he loved her. A strange thought now as he ponders when Amber was the last thing he thought about until now.

"He's stable, but we have to move, get the operating room prepped. Okay, bring in the wife." The doctor says as he removes his procedure mask.

Ryan hears the swinging door of the emergency room as it violently opens and also hears the shuffling of hurried steps toward him. He looks around, and Amber appears. She is crying and can barely speak. She reaches down and places her hands on his face. "Oh my God, baby...I love you...I love you."

"I love you too." Ryan mutters, "I am going to be okay don't worry."

"We have to go." the doctor yells.

"Wait just one more minute!" Amber screams.

"I'm sorry we have to go. He will be fine, let's go!" the doctor yells.

Amber is pulled away by the nurses, grasping at Ryan's arm, the smear of her fingertips visible on his skin from the blood she got on her hands from Ryan's face, as she continues pulling at the blood-stained blanket and screaming to Ryan. "I love you! I will be right here...I will be right here!" Amber collapses to the floor, clutching her face in her hands, the blood from Ryan's blood now transferred from her hands to her cheeks as she cries out uncontrollably.

A nurse in the room crouches down beside Amber and tries to comfort her. "He is going to be all right," the nurse whispers. "He is going to be all right."

The wait for Amber is excruciating as the hours pass with no word from anyone as to what is happening. Amber is surrounded by friends and family who have all arrived to lend their support. The mood is somber, and Amber struggles to remain still and continues to pace the narrow corridor and asks anyone who comes by if there is any news. Finally the operating room door opens. The doctor comes out pulling off his surgical gown and removing his procedure mask. He has no expression on his face and looks exhausted. Amber approaches him, holding a tissue in both hands.

"Is he okay?"

The doctor looks down at the floor and then glances up. "He is alive."

Amber breathes a sigh of relief; "However," the doctor begins to say.

"However what?"

"Ryan is in a coma."

"For how long?" Amber asks.

"I don't know, it could be a few days, several weeks, or…" Amber looks at the doctor with tear-filled eyes, "Or he may never wake up," the doctor says.

Amber breaks down in tears and begins to faint as family members rush to catch her. The feeling in the room is as if someone removed all the oxygen and replaced it with nothing.

Luke, who is Ryan's older brother, turns to the doctor and says, "Thank you doctor."

"We will do everything we can. I'm very sorry." the doctor says.

Luke just nods and returns his attention to Amber.

In the room, Ryan is looking around but notices that his eyes are closed. He calls out, but the echo of his voice carries nowhere, it is as if the sound was being removed the second it was noticed. Ryan begins to move, he knows that he is not physically moving but can still feel the sensation under his feet. He can see something familiar, the opening, the light. The excitement he feels is instantaneous, the same opening from the dream that first brought him to Sara. He hurriedly moves toward it. He can hear the waves crashing against the shore…his heart begins to race. *I'm back*, he thinks, *I'm back*. He looks out on the beach, the same sandy white beach; in the distance he sees one more familiar thing.

"Sara…" he whispers.

Suddenly Sara begins to run toward him, jumping into his arms, and as Ryan lifts her off the ground and twirls her around in happiness. "I knew you would come back." Sara states, "I knew it."

Ryan presses his lips against hers and stares into her eyes. "Yes, I'm back," he replies. "I'm back."

As he lets her feet hit the soft sand, he gazes at her and says, "You are all I have thought of." But in all his excitement Ryan has not even stopped thinking of how he has returned to Sara, only that he is happy that he has.

Sara looks back at Ryan and says, "I would have waited forever."

"I would have searched forever."

Sara reaches out and touches Ryan's face with the back of her hand and says, "I told you, love will always find a way."

Ryan pulls her close and with a passionate kiss he closes his eyes.

CHAPTER
FOUR

Ryan opens his eyes slowly; hesitant to gaze upon what might or might not be in front of him. What if it was all a dream, which is ironic because a dream is what started all of this, he thinks. Ryan can hear the weight of his own breath, the sound of which was like that of the *Star Wars* character Darth Vader, the sound so clear, it is as if he was standing next to him. Ryan cannot keep his eyes closed any longer, through the slits of his eyes, the blur turns to clarity as the shoreline becomes apparent. Ryan pauses, a strange sigh of relief comes over him. *Sara...*he wonders as a moment of panic comes over him. Suddenly he feels a familiar pressure on his hand as Sara squeezes it gently. Ryan's head instinctively turns to the source of the sensation. Sara smiles and looks down at the sand; she softly makes a small line in the sand with her foot. Ryan smiles and squeezes her hand.

"Hi," Ryan says, an almost childlike look on his face, it is as if he is looking at the world through the eyes of a child who is experiencing something for the first time and needs help understanding what to do.

Sara looks off in the distance and says, "Now, it is just you and I."

As they slowly start to walk along the beach, Ryan is now enjoying the tingly sensation of the sand between his toes as it brings him back to thinking how this is even possible. Ryan says nothing to Sara, but that thought and thousands more like it are racing through his mind and they are heavy. *Forget that, this can't be real*, he argues with himself with no one to debate the other side. *I'm here, I want to be here*, he thinks. Sara looks at Ryan, she can see his distant stare and the heaviness of his thoughts.

Sara pulls his attention toward her and with her free hand clutches his forearm. "Come on." she whispers. "We are here and that's all that matters now." she whispers.

The solitude of this spot on the beach is surreal. He thinks of the Manuel Antonio Beach in Costa Rica where he and Amber vacationed. The sound of the waves and the slight breeze lend to the thought. After a short walk the two find themselves sitting in the sand; they both stare out into the distance, the water slowly rolling in and back out to the sea. Sara clutches his arm and places her head on his shoulder, her eyes fixated.

She seems to be looking at something, as Ryan softly asks, "What are you looking at?"

Sara lifts her head off of his shoulder, a strange look on her face that becomes noticeably troublesome. "Sometimes I see people I knew…like shadows." she says, "Sometimes they seem like they are trying to speak to me…I can hear them far away, but I can't understand what they are saying."

Ryan has no reply to her comment, after all what answer could he give her when he himself is unable to understand what is happening? Ryan, looking out into the ocean, says, "This isn't real, you know that right?" His voice cracks slightly as he holds back his emotions.

Sara turns and looks toward Ryan. "Why, because you don't understand it?"

"And you do?"

"No, I don't understand it…I don't want to understand it, whatever this is. Wherever we are, I found you and you found me, that is what I know to be real. To think that I found happiness, in which I feel whole and safe, yet I have no idea what all of this is, and I'm so scared of losing it."

Ryan pulls Sara close and comforts her. "I'm sorry." he whispers, "I'm sorry." as he wipes the tears from her cheek as he helps her up.

Sara wipes the tears from her cheek and gets to her feet. "Let's go home." Sara says.

"Home?" Ryan replies. "Where is home?"

Sara giggles as she pulls Ryan along and begins running along the beach.

"Where are we going?" Ryan asks.

Sara doesn't answer and continues to run, pulling him along. Ryan is struggling to keep up. Finally as Sara's pace slows, Ryan looks in the distance as the shape of a small structure comes into view. It is a cottage, and as it becomes clearer, he can see that it strangely looks lived in. Sara pulls Ryan onto the grassy area in front of the cottage a few chairs and a quaint little table sit just outside the front door. The off-white paint of the exterior of the cottage seems like an odd choice. *But then isn't all of this odd?* he thinks. Ryan continues to look around; he can't help but think that he has seen this cottage before, in a magazine perhaps. The weathered look of it seems as if it has been here a long time and the unusual décor are items you might find at a garage sale but they added to the charm. The feel of the cottage and location is like something out of a romance novel, a romantic hideaway nestled in the jungle where the two characters from the story wish they could spend the rest of their lives.

As Ryan steps onto the porch, he can see the items placed there appear to be worn; it is as if the wear of time had left its mark from their constant use. Ryan focuses on the small living area he can see in the open doorway as Sara coaches him through the front door. Ryan looks around the area is decorated with simple furniture and knickknacks. A strange odor fills the room, it smells like a hospital or doctor's office. Ryan thinks it to be strange but dismisses the odor and says nothing to Sara.

"Do you like it?" Sara asks.

Ryan pauses with a puzzled look on his face. "I love it."

Sara moves to what looks to be a small kitchen. "Make yourself at home," Sara says as she approaches the counter.

Ryan slowly moves across the floor, hesitant but curious. An object above the mantle catches his attention, a handmade embroidered sign, it is the kind, Ryan thinks of tapestry a grandmother would make or own. He moves closer to it, his curiosity peaked as he tries to make out what it reads: "Love always finds a way."

"Did you make this?" Ryan asks as he remembers that it was something Sara said to him on the beach.

"No, it was a gift, I think?"

Sara moves to where Ryan is standing. Ryan unaware she is there, is startled when she wraps her arms around him. Ryan breaks from his thought regarding the embroidery, turns, and embraces Sara, looking over her shoulder at the small living area where Sara has brought him. His mind is exhausted from continuing to try to make sense of it all. He is haunted by the thousands of questions in his mind that appear to have no answers.

Sara pulls back slightly from Ryan, her hands still clutched around his waist. She looks up at him and says, "It will be dark soon, we will need to get some sleep."

"Sleep...we sleep?" Ryan thinks.

Sara leads Ryan to a small bed situated in the back of the cottage. Ryan takes a quick look around as they enter the room; his attention is directed to a small nightstand by the bed, this because of an unusual tiki statue placed on it. Sara seductively walks toward the bed, leading Ryan by the tips of her fingers against his outstretched arm. Ryan suddenly feels a sharp pain in his right arm, he pulls his arm away from Sara and stops sharply. His mind is aware of the sensation he felt but it does not match the action by Sara. Ryan reaches for the spot on his arm where he felt the pain, it is as if someone jabbed him with a needle, and the location is in the crook of his arm. Ryan looks down at his arm. His memory is telling him that he felt this sensation before and that it is the spot where a nurse would draw blood. Ryan rubs the area and stares at the spot but can see nothing, his mind searches for answers. He rubs it again trying to make sense of it.

Sara looks at Ryan, "Are you okay?"

Ryan continuing to rub his arm, looks up at Sara, "I'm fine… Yes, I'm fine."

Sara reaches to Ryan and pulls him toward her, her leg folded beneath her butt as she settles onto the bed. Sara reaches up and slowly lifts Ryan's shirt, her hands caressing his stomach as she gently kisses it. Ryan looks down as Sara glances up, a small strand of hair lays over her cheek, Ryan softly pushes it from her face. As they stare at one another, he feels as if he should feel guilty, after all he is married to Amber, but that feeling is absent, and a feeling of comfort and peace has taken its place. Sara pulls him onto the bed, Ryan gently falling atop her, his leg draped across her body. Ryan looks at Sara and rubs the back of his hand against her face. He caresses her cheek and runs his fingers across her lips. Sara closes her eyes and enjoys the sensation of Ryan's fingers as they gently move over her. He leans forward, and their lips meet, the tingly feel of her skin beneath his fingers as he softly touches her face, is prodigious. Although he has never been here, Ryan cannot shake the feeling of familiarity of the bed and the way the lights are illuminating the room. It almost has the appearance of a lowly lit waiting room at a doctor's office.

He breaks from his thought as Sara pulls his shirt over his head. Ryan pulls at Sara's blouse, lifting it and exposing her breasts. He stares at her milky white skin, small areolas, and the way Sara's chest is moving as she is breathing. Sara's movement is becoming less hesitant and more rapid as her excitement builds. Their clothing slowly becoming discarded items on the ground, creating less of a barrier as their bodies now touch against each other. Sara looks into Ryan's eyes, the anticipation of what is to come next is overwhelming, she tilts her head back and gasps as Ryan penetrates her, the slight pain quickly turns to the feeling of silkiness as her body welcomes what is happening. Sara pulls Ryan close, her hands firmly grasping the back of his arms, her legs lifted freely moving before wrapping themselves over Ryan's lower legs pulling him tighter and deeper inside herself.

The slow motion of their efforts becomes more labored as they feel the sensation of a physicality that they should not be able to feel.

Sara's legs move to wrap around Ryan's waist, each thrust ignites a passionate outcry from Sara. All motion stops as their bodies climax in ecstasy, Ryan looks down at Sara, the perspiration glistening on her skin as she quivers. Their labored breathing becomes shallower as they settle into staring at each other. Sara is gently caressing Ryan's back, her legs becoming more relaxed and settling against his. Ryan moves off of Sara onto his back as Sara rolls toward him and lays her head and hand against his chest. Ryan stares at the ceiling. *It is unusually plain and white*, almost like the ceiling in a building more than in a home he thinks. The thought quickly subsides as enjoys the calm feeling he is now experiencing.

As they drift off to sleep, Ryan suddenly hears a faint voice calling out to Sara. Ryan sits up and stares into the darkness, the voice seems so real but very faint. Out of the corner of his eye, he sees a shadowy figure, then another. They are different in shapes and sizes and appear to be pacing the room. He can't make them out but feels as if he knows them. He remembers what Sara said on the beach about the voices and shadows that she experienced. Ryan shakes his head and lays back down, his arm draped over his head. He looks over at Sara so peacefully asleep, while he is restless still unable to make sense of any of this. He focuses on the embroidery on the mantle, through its reflection in the long mirror in the room, "Love will find a way." Ryan's eyes are now heavy, he struggles to keep his eyes open before losing the battle and drifting off to sleep.

Ryan finds himself thinking of Amber as his consciousness fades; it is almost as if he can hear her talking and softly crying. He cannot shake the sensation that Amber is in the room and touching his arm and hand. Ryan can only think that it is the guilt of what has happened between him and Sara and how insane it is to feel guilt over a dream that has no basis in reality. He dismisses the feeling as Sara snuggles against him; he stares at Sara's body through the faint light coming through the window. He has never felt this way, well maybe in the beginning of his marriage to Amber, but that was a long time ago he thinks, *What did I know about that then?* he ponders to himself. Ryan now thinking that he is "Asleep" but continues to hear the voices in the room. He looks around but can see no one. None of the voices Ryan can hear now are familiar all but one, and one he knows very well…Amber.

Ryan is trying to convince himself that the voices he hears and in particular Amber's, is a product of his imagination or of the guilt he feels, a reminder that she, unlike Sara, is real. As the voices move about the room, he notices that he is alone, Sara is not there. *But Sara was next to me,* he thinks, *none of this is making any sense.* "Sara," he whispers, "Where are you?" As he looks around the room, the one thing that is unmistakable is the sound of sadness and despair in the voices he is hearing. Ryan knows this is all related but continues to tell himself that it isn't, as he continues to search for Sara.

Suddenly he can feel a pull at his arm. He quickly turns and sees that Sara is looking at him,

"Good morning." She says.

"Good morning," Ryan says as he takes a breath, "What happened to you?" he asks, "You were gone, where did you go?"

"I don't know." Sara replies, "I could not find you either but I knew you were still here somewhere."

Sara leans against his chest, "I have never been this happy." She says seemingly unconcerned by what just happened.

Ryan looks toward Sara and replies, "Neither have I." Ryan is still shaken from the experience but sees that Sara is okay and once again by his side, so he dismisses it and continues on.

They both get out of bed and move to a small table just off the living room. As they both sit for a moment, Ryan notices that there are no familiar sounds or smells the morning might bring—the smell of coffee or the sound of bacon cooking. Ryan looks up at Sara and asks, "Do we eat?—Do we drink?"

Sara pauses and says, "Let's go down to the beach." Ignoring Ryan's question.

"Okay, we will, but please answer me."

"I haven't…I don't know. Can we go now?"

Ryan senses that his question has troubled Sara and she is visibly uneasy. *Maybe she doesn't know*, Ryan thinks. *How can I expect her to when I don't understand it myself?* Ryan takes Sara's hand and leads her toward the front door. Sara walks then abruptly stops, jerking Ryan to a standstill.

Sara looks at Ryan and tells him, "No, we don't eat…We don't drink. I don't know how this is all possible, but there is something I have to tell you." There is a long pause as Ryan stares at Sara not knowing what she is about to say. "What? …what is it?" Ryan asks. Sara takes a breath and hesitantly says, "I have a husband." Ryan pauses and says "A husband?" "Yes." Sara replies "I can still hear him and sometimes feel like he is here. I did not want to tell you." Sara says as she begins to cry.

Ryan stares, pauses but says nothing, this due to the fact that he is experiencing the same things and that he too has a wife. Ryan with a mix of emotion from sadness to joy pulls Sara toward him, and with both hands clutching behind her triceps, he tells Sara that he is experiencing the same things and that he, too, has a wife. Then Sara with almost a look of relief on her face asks.

"What is her name?" Sara asks.

"Amber." Ryan replies.

Sara pauses as a single tear wells up in her eye and runs down her face. "My husband's name is Albert."

Ryan looks at Sara "I don't know why all this is happening, and I don't know how long it will last, but like you said, we are here now and that is all that matters." Ryan wipes the tear from Sara's cheek, her eyes filled with a strange mixture of sadness and comfort.

As the two walk outside together and stand on the porch that overlooks the beach, Ryan asks, "Do you want to go back if you could?"

Sara, without turning toward Ryan replies, "At first it was all I could think of, and I did not want to be alone. Then one day you came here, wherever here is." Sara says with frustration mixed with happiness. "Now all I want is to be here with you."

Ryan places his arm around Sara's shoulder and pulls her close. "Me too," Ryan whispers and continues to stare out over the water. "We can have a life here, even though we don't understand everything that is happening."

"We can adjust…We can make this our world," Sara whispers.

"I already have," Ryan replies. "I already have," he says again as he tightens his hold of Sara.

"This place and you are now the only world I want," Sara proclaims, "And for as long as it last's, I will be here by your side."

Ryan looks to Sara and smiles. "I promise, for as long as we are here, I will love you."

Sara quickly turns to Ryan. "You love me?"

"Yes, I know it is crazy but I love you. You're everything I have ever wanted and have ever wanted to feel with another person."

Sara places her hands on Ryan's face and pulls their faces together, and with a deep sigh, tells Ryan, "I love you too, more than I thought was even possible. I was so lost and alone before I came here, and I cannot understand why I feel more love and comfort here than where I was, and I am so scared that whatever power brought us here will eventually take it away."

Ryan looks at Sara, "I'm scared too. I don't want to fall asleep, afraid that I might wake up, and you won't be there. All I want to do is to be standing right here looking at you and wondering how someone like me could find someone like you and if I even deserve it enough to stay." Ryan states.

Sara's hand moves down Ryan's forearm, her fingers interlacing his fingers; the pulse of their collective heartbeats is profound. Sara reaches with her free hand and lightly places it on his bicep. "I have waited so long for something like this, I want so much the same thing you want, to remain here by your side and love you with all that I have. I promise no matter how long we have, I will love you. I love you, Ryan," Sara says, "I love you." "This is us now, this is our new life, wherever we are." Ryan replies.

As the two of them commit to one another, both Ryan and Sara secretly and collectively think of Albert and Amber and the life they both have left behind. Ryan squeezes Sara's hand as the two look out to the world they now call home.

CHAPTER
FIVE

What seems like months have now gone by and Ryan and Sara could not be happier. Their days are filled with laughter and long conversations that play out each of their lives in wide detail. They have both lost sight of the reality of where they were and how they came to be here. They both go on as if this new "life" was a fresh start, a chance to set things right, a chance to have the love they both have searched for their whole lives, while ignoring that this new found reality is filled with uncertainty and completely out of their control. At the end of a long day and as the sun begins to set, the two settle in for another night of comfort and their insatiable passion for each other.

In the darkness, Ryan, for the first time sees that Sara is restless, her seemingly uncomfortable twitching alerts something deep inside of him that something is not quite right. Ryan feels a strange warmth come over him, not a sensation of temperature so to speak, but more of an emotional sensation. At that moment, Ryan begins to feel what he thinks is pain… "Why pain?" he asks himself, a slight feeling of panic comes over him.

In a nervous voice, Ryan whispers, "Sara," his uneasy nervousness turns to urgency as he touches her on the shoulder…"Sara." he whispers again.

Sara awakens and asks, "Are you okay?"

"I don't know." Ryan whispers, as he looks around the room with panic and confusion, trying to compose himself.

Sara sits up and is becoming concerned, her face and actions begin to reflect that concern as she stares and reaches to Ryan with panic. Ryan suddenly feels a sharp pain in the crutch of his right arm, a familiar pain that he has felt before. He gasps and cries out, "SARA!"

Sara reaches out to him. "Baby! …Baby!" she cries.

Her voice begins to fade. Ryan's view of her face begins to narrow; he struggles to get his bearing. Suddenly the darkness opens up to light. Ryan opens his eyes slightly, the light barely piercing through the small slits in his eyes he has allowed himself to see through. For a moment he is relieved; as the feel of the bed and the light of the room and even the smells are familiar as the smells of the cottage are unmistakable. He takes a breath. The air feels heavy, and a feeling of pain comes over him. Ryan looks around in terror. "Where am I?" Ryan whispers. *Where is Sara?* He thinks as he tries to adjust his eyes to the light and scans down his body at the bedding; he can see his arm, and there is something sticking out of it, at first this makes no sense, then, as he gathers his wits he thinks, *Of course it is an IV, a hospital,* he thinks, and in looking at the sheets it confirms what he is thinking. *That's impossible,* he thinks, he has seen enough. A fear that he has never felt before in his life has now completely consumed him and he is trembling like a shivering dog left out in the rain.

He cries out, "SARA!"

A voice replies, "I'm here." For a moment his panic subsides until he realizes that it is not Sara's voice; he struggles in his mind to recognize the voice. He turns his head to the direction of the voice as he desperately tries to focus on the face. In doing so his breathing has become labored and as he continues to struggle he is becoming more and more frightened. Slowly a face comes into view and he can feel the sensation of someone taking his hand, as the voice begin to scream, "Help, someone help…he is awake!"

"I'm here." the voice states again.

The face and the voice are now clear, it is Amber. Ryan shakes his head in disbelief as Amber looks down at him. Her eyes swollen from the fatigue and sadness she has endured for the last several months.

"Where am I?" Ryan asks.

"You are in the hospital, you had an accident." Amber replies and pauses, and with a look of confusion, asks, "Who is Sara?"

"What?" Ryan replies.

"When you woke up and opened your eyes, you called out Sara."

Ryan struggles to come up with an answer that makes sense, all the while trying to understand what is happening. Ryan hastily mutters, "Sara."—"I don't know a Sara."

Amber firmly grasps Ryan's hand. Ryan gently squeezes back as the room becomes clearer. Ryan fixates on the face of Amber whose tear-filled eyes and quivering lip let him know that he is back...back to a life of reality. The sounds of rushing orderlies echo in the room as the news of his awakening becomes known. Ryan stares at the ceiling, the voice of a man he is not familiar with is speaking.

"Ryan, I am Dr. Miles. Can you tell me where you are?"

Ryan struggles to understand the question as the light of a small penlight waves back and forth across his eyes, the slight pressure of someone holding open his eye lids is uncomfortable. "I am in the hospital?" Ryan replies.

"Yes, you are in the hospital. You have been in a coma."

"How long have I been here?"

"Three months." the doctor replies.

Ryan looks away, as a single tear rolls down his cheek. A strange feeling of sadness looms over him, but he is not crying in gratitude to have awaken from his coma, or to be able to see Amber again but the sadness over the separation between him and Sara, he knows Sara is gone!

Ryan's recovery is a slow and painful process. The accident has limited his ability to move his legs. *And what if this is permanent?* he thinks. Amber is a constant fixture in the room and although Ryan is grateful and knows it is her love that keeps her at his side, while at the same time he is almost annoyed at her presence. He feels guilty in feeling that way about Amber but the guilt he feels fails in comparison to the pain he feels being there without Sara. The constant parade of staff in and out of the room is trying and in some cases frustrating. He knows that they are there to help, but he wishes they would all just leave. Ryan finds himself snapping at them in frustration. The constant guilt of behaving that way rests heavily upon him, seemingly admonishing him for his behavior. The days and nights are so long, each night he closes his eyes anticipating a possible reunion with Sara and every morning opens them defeated as that reunion never comes. Ryan's hopes fade as each passing day slips away with nothing more than a memory of Sara's face.

Each day Amber can be found sitting at the chair beside his bed. He loves her for that, her kind words of encouragement and the unexpected soft touches are comforting. He begins to hate himself for feeling the way he does and for missing out on what he has instead wanting something in his mind. He struggles within himself as he forces himself not to forget whatever it was that he shared with Sara, and to focus on what he has before him. The pain overtime is becoming less and less, and the visible scars are beginning to be the only record of the ordeal that he suffered.

Ryan awakens to the sound of medical staff moving about the room. Amber comes into view, and his eyes focus on the feeling of her hair on his arm. "Ryan," Amber whispers, "you have a visitor."

Ryan looks around the room as far as his line of sight will allow him. "Who?" Ryan asks.

Amber moves slowly to one side, offering a glimpse of the door. Ryan can see a figure; he takes a deep breath, and his heart begins to race and a cold sweat comes over him. *Sara*, he thinks. The figure begins to move closer, his mind racing.

"Ryan." the figure says.

Ryan realizes that the voice is familiar, but it is not Sara; a mixture of relief and sadness comes over him. *What would I say to Amber if it was Sara?* He thinks.

"Ryan," the voice mutters again.

Ryan realizes that it is Charlie and as he becomes clearer in Ryan's eyes, he sees tears running down his face.

"I am so sorry." The shakiness of Charlie's voice can be felt more than heard. His hands wringing the worn-out baseball cap that he wore every day.

Ryan struggles to smile and tells Charlie in a just-awakened voice, "You really need to learn how to drive."

Charlie smiles ever so slightly, a visible look of relief falls over him. Charlie moves closer, and again apologizes.

"We're good, my friend," Ryan says "We're good" as he chokes up and tears fill his eyes.

"How are you doing?" Charlie asks.

"I am going to be okay."

Amber is looking down at Ryan, the tears streaming down her face, her hand gripping Ryan's hand firmly. The emotion is so strong Ryan can feel it in her touch. The sweat of her hand triggers a memory of the first time he and Amber held hands as a young couple, just two kids madly in love, unsure but so excited. In that instance, he looks at Amber, he is startled as he sees Sara smiling back at him. He closes his eyes, tightly, his mind telling him *Do not open your eyes* but his emotions are too much, he opens his eyes and sees it is Amber. Ryan nods his head as Amber smiles and asks, "You okay?"

Ryan takes a breath and swallows the lump in his throat. "I'm fine." Ryan replies "It's just a lot."

"It's okay. I just thought I would come by and see you, I best be getting going." Charlie says.

"No, it's okay. I am glad you came by, please stay."

"No, I best be getting on and let you rest. I will come back later on."

Ryan just nods, the feeling of sorrow for what Charlie must be feeling as he watches him leave the room; he silently and oddly thanks Charlie. He knows that without him and what happened, he would have not had the time he spent with Sara.

The silence of his thoughts is interrupted as Amber again asks, "Are you okay?"

Ryan turns toward Amber, his eyes filled with tears. "I'm okay. I just feel bad for Charlie."

Amber smiles and says to Ryan, "You are a good man. Most people would be furious at someone who did this to them."

Ryan just smiles and takes the misplaced compliment and thinks to himself, *You are an asshole.*

Time is moving along. Ryan's strength is returning, and he has gotten up several times a day for physical therapy. The pain in his body is bearable unlike the pain in his heart. Amber looks on and has no idea that the sound of his wrenching and gasping has little to do with the physical pain that he is experiencing. Each day becomes an experience in getting better and feeling worse. The doctors, nurses, and physical therapist are all amazed at the progress that Ryan is making as well as his sheer determination. What everyone doesn't realize is that the motivation is the beautiful dream he had and his need to find answers and try to get back there. Ryan has it in his mind that if he can get well enough, he can figure out what happened and how he can get back to Sara. He thinks that Sara is probably feeling the same and is searching for him as well. These thoughts have completely consumed him, and even though Amber is by his side, he overlooks her efforts and her physical reality; he only wishes for the dream to return.

Ryan is unable to shake the feeling that somehow Sara is real, and even though he does not understand what happened, the feelings he has for Sara have become so powerful. He thinks that he must get back, there has to be a way back. Ryan's recovery is almost complete.

Amber is so excited, and she has been making plans for weeks now for Ryan's return home. "Everything is ready. I have gotten everything the doctor has recommended, and I can't wait for you to see it." She says.

Ryan smiles and half-heartedly thanks Amber telling her, "I don't need everything they are telling you, I am fine. I don't want all this fuss, it is too much." Before he realizes it, he has changed his tone from thankfulness to annoyance. He doesn't notice right away, but Amber has stopped talking and is now looking at him with bewilderment and sadness. Ryan tries to cover it. "I'm sorry," he says, "I am just tired. Thank you. You have really done a lot, and I am so grateful you are here."

Amber smiles, "It's okay. I know you are going through a lot." She replies.

"I don't mean to take it out on you." Ryan responds.

"It's okay, I am here no matter what."

"I know." Ryan says.

He is so sad and conflicted inside. Here he has a beautiful wife in the flesh who has been by his side, through it all and yet all his thoughts are to the beautiful woman of his dreams who has taken a place in his heart that Amber has never occupied. He knows it is wrong and tries to push out the memories of Sara, but her warm touch is not easily forgotten. Ryan awakens to the sound of hustle and bustle of the nursing staff. The day has come. It is time to go home. He looks down at the floor and sees that Amber has packed everything up in plastic bags. *Well I am homeless.* He thinks with a small laugh but his humor quickly becomes abated as the thought of going back to a home he is now sharing with someone other than the woman he loves definitely makes him homeless.

Amber approaches the bed. "Good morning, babe," Amber joyfully says. "Let's get you ready to go. I'll bet you can't wait to get out of here." As she moves around the room gathering Ryan's things, "Please let me know when you're ready."

"Okay, I'm ready" Ryan replies as Amber hurries over to help him to the edge of the bed. Amber begins to help Ryan put on his t-shirt, when Ryan proclaims "I can dress myself."

"Okay." Amber replies as she steps back all the while watching.

Ryan struggles to put the clothes on.

"Are you sure?" she asks.

Ryan with his arm caught in the T-shirt, his face buried in the tangled garment, and in a ridged tone states, "Yes, I'm sure."

Ryan manages to get his shirt on just in time to see the orderly come into the room. Ryan just looks at the wheelchair that the orderly has brought with him, *Really,* he thinks, "I don't think I need a wheelchair." he says under his breath but he has no choice because it is of course hospital policy. Ryan shuffles to the wheelchair, Amber lingering over him and assisting him unnecessarily, which is beginning to irritate Ryan. As the wheelchair glides down the hallway, the staff looks on and wishes him well. He feels bad for those who have to stay, especially those in the hallway that he just passed, a wing of the hospital he is very familiar with; this is the wing he was in when he was in his coma. *Those patients are in a coma*, he thinks, *they may never be getting out of here.*

As he proceeds down the hallway, a disheveled and tired-looking man stands in the hallway and watches Ryan as he passes. Ryan makes eye contact with the man, and remembers feeling so bad for him. Ryan debates on if he should say something, and if he did, what would he say? Ryan decides to just look away as he passes. As he makes his way past the man, he catches a glimpse of a blonde woman lying on the bed in the room, tropical flowers in the vase, a strange tiki figure on the nightstand, and a handmade sign over the bed which looked like some type of an embroidery. Ryan tries to read what it says but can only make out "Love Will" something as the orderly whisks him by the room. Ryan can also see as he passes the room what could be family and friends of the woman who are gathered around the bed, and fill the room.

His wife…I'll bet that is his wife, Ryan thinks of the man he just passed in the hallway, how horrible that is, and with that thought, looks up at Amber and reaches for her hand. Ryan gives Amber's hand a gentle tug. Amber looks down at him and smiles as they approach the entrance. The doors swing open, and the first gush of outside air consumes him. He revels in the feel of the sun now firmly upon him and is thankful to be outside and alive. Amber had already taken the time and initiative to drive the truck to the door that morning, and it was now waiting to take him home. The orderly and Amber help him out of the wheelchair and into the passenger seat of the truck, Ryan struggles and lets out a loud sigh as he settles in. Ryan watches as Amber walks around the front of the truck and gets in. Amber turns to Ryan smiles and says, "Are you ready?" Ryan smiles back, and says, "Let's go home." Amber starts the truck, places it in drive and pulls away.

Ryan looks back at the hospital as it fades in the rearview mirror, *I am going home…* Ryan thinks to himself, while feeling a strange mixture of thoughts and emotions. In part he is thankful that he has made it this far, somber as he knows a part of him will forever live in that place. He feels sadness for the man in the hallway and finally the guilt and shame he feels knowing that he is leaving there with his wife and how lucky he is to be able to do so, meanwhile wishing he was somewhere else with someone else. He is disgusted with himself, and with complete feeling of loathing, turns to Amber.

"Thank you." he whispers.

"For what?" Amber asks.

"For being here."

Amber smiles. "Of course, I love you."

Ryan smiles as he now knows that he is the worst person in the world. He looks down at the floor and then back to Amber. "I don't deserve you." he mutters.

Amber looks at Ryan and smiles; she says nothing in return and offers only a look of completeness. Ryan pulls his baseball cap over his eyes and settles his head between the window and the head rest, as he stares out of the window he can't help but compare the swift-moving landscape to the thoughts racing through his mind.

CHAPTER
SIX

The thought passes through Ryan's mind of how the drive from the hospital is so long, while in the same instance how slow time was passing now. He can hear the beating of his heart like the sound of a train passing through the mountains in the distance, but just as he becomes restless the sound of the gravel being moved by the tires of the truck tires is an obvious sign, they are home. Ryan watches as Amber comes around to the passenger side of the truck. Ryan struggles to turn himself in the direction of the door to get out. Amber gently reaches for his arm. "I got you." Amber whispers. "Come on." she says.

Ryan plants his feet on the gravel of the driveway, the sound of the gravel solidifies that he is home. Ryan drapes his arm over Amber's shoulder as they slowly move across the driveway towards the porch, on their way to the front door. *Everything looks the same,* Ryan thinks as he scans his surroundings. The climb up the porch steps is a slow process; Ryan steadies himself on the rail as Amber helps him along. As they cross the porch, Buddy looks up at Ryan, a strange look on his face, it is a look of recognition but at the same time a look of abandonment.

"Hey boy!" Ryan calls out, Buddy, with his head raised, doesn't move, his tail intermittently wagging. "Hey boy," Ryan calls out again "Come here!"

However, Buddy is still without any sudden movement and continues to stare. Suddenly his tail begins to wag more frantically and with a sudden jolt gets to his feet and makes his way to Ryan. Ryan chokes up as his eyes fill with tears. "How are you boy?… That's a good boy." Ryan says.

Buddy is now wiggling and panting with excitement as he brushes up against Ryan. "Let's go inside boy."

Amber looks on, her eyes are also filled with tears as they make their way inside with Buddy in tow. *The house looks the same,* Ryan thinks again, not knowing why he thought it would look different. Amber helps him to the couch. "Is this okay?" Amber asks.

"Yes, this is good." as he settles onto the couch.

Amber places her things on the counter and tells Ryan, "Let me make you something to eat."

"No, I'm fine." Ryan replies.

"You are probably starving."

"I'm fine." Ryan says again, this time with an elevated tone.

Amber dismisses Ryan and begins to rummage through the kitchen. Ryan grabs the remote to turn on the TV but hesitates turning it on. He stares at the blank screen and thinks of Sara, and as he stares at the TV, remote in hand, he fades deeper into his thought; then with a sudden jerk, his body reacts to Amber standing in front of him.

"Are you going to turn that on?" Amber asks. "What are you thinking about?"

Ryan sighs and turns on the TV. "Nothing, why?" He says.

Amber stands there for a moment, a strange look on her face as if she is trying to figure out what he is thinking about as she hands Ryan a small plate of food and a napkin. "You can take a nap, after you eat, you're probably tired." Amber states as she turns and walks back to the kitchen.

As the days wear on, the unmistakable feeling of something is missing is consuming him. It is the feeling of being out of place along with the uncomfortable sensation in his neck running along his chest and into his stomach that seems to be a constant companion now. Ryan feels so guilty, his blatant disregard toward Amber, a love that has stood beside him through everything, meanwhile all of his attention directed to someone who lives in his dreams. The thought of choosing the physical love of the person who has been with him daily, over someone that is a dream is crazy even to him.

Amber enters the room. "Have you taken your pills today?" she asks.

Ryan, with hesitation, nods, with no clear indication if he meant yes or no. However Amber is relentless, a constant buzzing around him, wanting to make sure that he is okay. He knows that she is doing it out of love, but he can't stop the feeling of annoyance because of it; this coupled with the constant guilt of feeling that way, is a burden that Ryan is not sure how long he will be able to endure. Suddenly there is a knock at the door. Ryan sighs. He is unable to see who it is, then hears Amber say, "Come in." He is sure it is no one important but fears it could be yet another reminder of the reality he is living in. Ryan's intuition is correct and is a very harsh reminder of his reality, it is Amber's mother, Barbara.

"It's me!" she shouts through the screen door, her head moving from side to side, looking into the living room. "Hello!" she shouts. "Come in, I'm in the bedroom!" Amber yells.

Ryan makes no sound. Amber comes out of the bedroom and says, "Hi, Mom, I said come in." "Sorry, I didn't hear you." Barbara replies as Amber walks across the living room and opens the door and lets her in. Buddy makes no sudden movement; the familiar guest and his indifference sparks no interest within him. Buddy simply lifts his head slightly from his laying position by the couch then with a glance returns his head to the floor and sighs.

"How are you doing, Rye?" Barbara asks.

Why does she continue to call me Rye? Ryan thinks, *I never gave her permission to call me Rye,* but it is something she has done for as long as he has known her. Ryan looks straight ahead and says, "Better."

"That is so good to hear," Barbara says as she sits on the arm of the couch and taps Ryan on the hand.

Ryan smirks and thinks to himself of how fortunate he is for the invention of painkillers and muscle relaxers as he continues to watch the TV, not wanting to make eye contact while watching Barbara peripherally. Amber's mother, who was now trying to get into heaven after a lifetime of bad deeds and bad decisions, is sober and makes it a point to let everyone who will listen know how many days that is and how wonderful she is now. Barbara leaves Ryan's side and heads to the kitchen where Amber is. The sound of Barbara's voice screeches in the kitchen, telling Amber, "I am so happy, two years and three days sober... Thank God."

Which is ironic, Ryan thinks, *as God was not a factor until she was told by the doctor and the authorities that if she continued to drink, she would either end up dead or in jail.* Ryan laughs. *What an idiot,* he thinks to himself. Ryan listens as the two discuss his current state of health and progress as if he were not in the same room with them. Ryan hated the fact that her mother, who had never shown an interest in Amber's life nor their life together, suddenly has to be constantly briefed with the latest information regarding the two them, and his condition.

Ryan's mind wanders as Barbara's visit sparks memories and feelings in Ryan, he misses his father and mother. Ryan's mother, who passed away in November of the previous year at the age of eighty-four, was a constant reminder of what love was all about and how he could still feel that love in his soul. Ryan's father passing away several years earlier at the age of seventy was a different story as he had a difficult time expressing love. His father was a difficult man and he and Ryan did not always get along, but over the years Ryan came to accept that his father did the best he could with what he knew and Ryan was thankful for that. He can feel himself tearing up, but wants no part of the attention that he will receive from the two in the kitchen if those tears make it onto his cheeks. Ryan pinches his nose between his eyes and helps to stop the tears. Ryan shouts out, "I am going to bed now!"

Amber comes out to the living room. "Do you need help?" she asks.

"I got it." Ryan replies as he lifts himself to his feet, a cane at the ready. He does not necessarily need it, but it helps. *The help from Amber would be nice*, he thinks to himself but can't bear the thought of accepting that help knowing that Barbara would want to help too.

As he struggles to stand, Barbara screeches out from the kitchen. "Good night, Rye!"

Ryan just waves and mumbles. "Good night."

As Ryan makes his way down the hallway, he is optimistic. *Maybe tonight*, he thinks. Just maybe he will get to see Sara, which has not been the case since he returned home. *Maybe it was all just a dream*, he thinks or maybe it was time to accept the fact that he is home now and that is all there is. His optimism is dampened by the sadness of that possibility but continues on down the hallway. The only thing is Ryan can still feel the realness of Sara's presence; he knows that it is not like shadows and distant voices he heard when he was with Sara, *or could it be?* Ryan thinks.

Ryan makes his way into the bedroom and sits on the bed, taking off his shoes. The constant pain he is still in makes it so difficult to do the most simple of tasks. In frustration he throws one shoe across the room, the thud brings Buddy to the door. "It's okay, boy." Ryan says as Buddy gives Ryan a look of understanding before turning away and heading back to the living room. As Ryan watches Buddy walk away somehow one tear that he was holding back in the living room has fought its way to his cheek. Ryan sighs and gives up on removing his clothing. He lies back on the bed, and pulls the blanket over him, and drifts off to sleep.

As he falls into a deep sleep, he can hear a faint voice, it is familiar. He moves toward it as the voice is getting clearer. *It is Sara*, he excitingly thinks as he begins to move faster toward the sound. In the haze he finds himself trying to make out the faint outline of a person that can be seen through the mist. As the outline becomes more defined and less unobstructed, he knows it is her "Sara?"…it is Sara!

Ryan gasps and runs toward her at the same time Sara is also running toward Ryan and with a sudden impact they embrace. Each of them holding on for dear life, afraid to let go.

"Where have you been?" Ryan asks as he chokes back the tears.

"Right here." Sara replies, "Trying to find you."

As they continue to embrace, Ryan says, "I thought you were just a dream."

"No, I'm here," Sara replies. Ryan stares at Sara, he is happy but unsure of what happened that brought him back. "I don't know what is happening the voices and shadows I told you about, they wouldn't allow me to reach you," Sara says. "I was so scared that I was never going to break free."

Ryan holds Sara tight. "We are here now, that's what matters."

Sara is holding her head against his chest, her breathing labored from their exchange. Once they calm down they begin to walk along the beach. "Have you thought of why we are here and where this is?" Ryan asks.

"Yes, but it feels like I do not want to know," Sara replies. Ryan stares off into the distance thinking of Sara's reply, "I am terrified of knowing, I'm afraid I will lose you again if I knew everything. Maybe that is why we keep getting separated. We know too much!" Sara exclaims, Ryan pulls Sara close.

"You will never lose me." Ryan replies. "I don't want to know either for the same reasons, but maybe if we can figure this out, we can stay here." Ryan says.

Sara looks up at him and says, "What if it doesn't work and we find out we can't stay?"

Ryan holds onto Sara trying to reassure her everything will be okay. "I think we have to try." Ryan replies, "I can't go on not knowing what all of this is or that we may never know why all of this is happening to us."

As they make their way to the cottage, Ryan pushes the issue. "Do you remember anything?"

"Please stop." Sara replies, dismissing Ryan, walking ahead of him as they enter the cottage. "I don't want to do this right now." Sara mutters.

"Okay,…"Okay we don't have to." Ryan replies.

As they enter the bedroom, Ryan's attention is diverted as he looks to the nightstand by the bed and he sees a vase with newly pick flowers beautifully displayed. "How beautiful." Ryan mentions.

"Aren't they?" Sara replies. "They grow wild here." she tells Ryan, as she looks at them and touches them with her fingers. "I love this," Sara says as she picks up the small tiki statue which was next to the flowers.

Ryan walks closer to Sara and takes the small statue from her hands; he looks at it and asks, "Where did you get this?"

"I don't remember." Sara says, "but it's cute, right?" As she takes it back from Ryan and places it back on the nightstand, staring at it adoringly.

Ryan pauses and is troubled; he can't shake the feeling that he has seen those items before, but where? As Sara leads Ryan into the bedroom he suddenly feels a quick jerk of his arm. He looks down at his arm, then feels another jerk he quickly looks up at Sara as her image flickers with each tug, it is like he is looking at a hologram that is running out of power. Ryan frightened begins to utter in panic, "*No...no...no...Sara...Sara.*"

CHAPTER
SEVEN

The force of a last tug jerks Ryan awake. His eyes come open, and Amber is standing over him. "What the fuck!" Ryan screams. Amber looks at Ryan startled by his response. "Where am I?" Ryan asks.

"You're home." Amber replies, "You're home."

"Why did you wake me up, Amber?" Ryan asks, with anger in his voice.

"It looked like you were having a bad dream. Are you okay?" Amber asks as Ryan sits up and moves to the end of the bed.

"I'm fine," Ryan replies. "Don't ever wake me up like that again." Ryan lays back down on the bed, trying to control his heavy breathing from the ordeal. *Sara's gone again*, he thinks. And Amber is to blame, knowing that Amber has no idea what just happened.

Amber pauses, not knowing how to react and looking as if to ask, Did I do something wrong? But instead turns and goes back in to the kitchen. Ryan sighs with disappointment in himself for the way he treated Amber and total sadness for losing Sara again. Morning has come, Ryan makes his way to the kitchen, pulls out a chair from the kitchen table, and slowly sits down. Amber stares out of the small window above the kitchen sink, the silence is unmistakable. He knows that she is trying to understand. *But how do you understand something that you are not even aware of?* he thinks.

"Are we okay?" Amber asks without turning around, still staring out the window.

"Of course." Ryan replies. "Of course we are okay."

The rest of the morning goes on without incident and for now the previous night's events also go unmentioned. Later that morning, Ryan says to Amber, "I think I am going to go to the hospital."

"For what?…Are you okay?"

"I'm fine, I was thinking I just wanted to see and thank everyone at the hospital and I never got the chance to do that." Ryan replies.

"That sounds like a wonderful idea." Amber replies. "Do you want me to go with you?"

"No, it's okay." Ryan quickly replies.

"Okay." Amber says with a look of sadness on her face a feeling of being left out.

Ryan begins to make his way to the truck, with Buddy walking alongside. "Not today, Buddy," as he coaches Buddy away from the truck door. The sound of the engine brings Amber to the door, a small smile and a wave as Ryan pulls out of the driveway.

Driving to the hospital, Ryan's thoughts are racing. *Why is all of this happening?* As he pulls into the parking lot of the hospital, a feeling of dread comes over him, it is almost as if an invisible force is telling him to turn around and go home. As he exits the truck and slowly moves toward the hospital doors, the feeling of dread is getting stronger. As the doors slide open, Ryan walks through and as fate would have it, the first person in the hallway is the nurse who cared for him after he came out of his coma, Vanessa Smith, who was a bit of a talker but nice.

She quickly recognizes Ryan and excitingly greets him and gives him a hug. "How are you?" she asks.

Ryan smiles. "I'm fine."

"What are you doing here?" she asks.

"Just coming to see all of you and say thank you."

"Ahh," Vanessa mutters as a small gathering of the people who cared for him grows; all of them are smiling and happy to see his progress.

Ryan is appreciative and receptive as he shakes hands and gives hugs to the staff. In the commotion, Ryan glances down the hallway. "I think I will to go up to the coma ward and have a look around," he says, "It was great seeing all of you." He states.

Everyone smiles and wishes him well as he makes his way down the hallway. Ryan can't understand it but it is almost like he is unable to walk from the weight of dread that has plagued him from the parking lot. Ryan makes his way to the elevator and gets in the sound of the floor indicator seems especially loud today he thinks. As the elevator doors open, a rush of air hits him, and as he steps out the familiar odors are unmistakable, yet his mind is unable to understand why the familiarity between the smell he is experiencing and that of the cottage, *what is the connection of the two?* perhaps *it is just a lingering sensation from his dream perhaps?* He thinks then quickly dismisses the thought and makes his way through the hallway to the coma ward. As he passes the room he was in he can see the room where the blonde woman is, in the distance, Ryan makes his way closer and is able to see there is people in the room. For some unknown reason he wants to see the woman's face; however her face is still obscured by a breathing tube and pillow, her blonde hair is the only feature he can see, Ryan surmises it is the husband who is still perched in the doorway.

As Ryan approaches, the man who Ryan thinks is the husband looks at him with a look of familiarity. "You're the guy right?" Ryan stares in silence, "The guy that woke up from his coma? You were in the room down the hall, right?" the man asks.

"Yes." Ryan replies.

The man stretches out his arm and extends his hand. "I'm Albert, Albert Adams." he says.

Ryan stretches out his hand, "I'm Ryan, Ryan Allen." he replies in return. Albert's hands feel cold and empty as if his very soul was missing. "Is that your wife?" Ryan asks, "Yes." Albert replies "How long has she been that way? If you don't mind me asking." Ryan says.

"Since December first of this last year." Albert replies.

"December first?" Ryan asks as his breathing stops for a moment, a lump in his throat so big he feels as if he cannot swallow, as he tries to move to get a better look at the woman. Ryan's mind races as to the familiarity with that date. Ryan looks at Albert and says, "My accident was in December."

"Really?" Albert asks.

"Yes on the third." Ryan says then looks into the room, his mind is telling him, *This cannot be,* and feels himself becoming panicked. *This is insane,* Ryan says to himself, Albert looks at Ryan and says, "Now that is a coincidence." Ryan struggles to position himself to fully see the woman's face, without being obvious. "Yes that is quite a coincidence."

"It is crazy how things happen, you were in a work accident right?" Albert asks.

"Yes."

"In my wife's case, it was a car accident, she was thrown from the car, and barely survived." Albert says.

"Where did it happen?" Ryan asks.

"Out on Saw Mill Road, near mile marker 187."

"I live close to there."

"Do you?"

"Yes, maybe a mile if not closer."

"Small world." Albert states.

"Absolutely." Ryan replies as he is slowly moving around Albert, trying to get a better view of the woman in the room without drawing attention to the what he is doing. Ryan suddenly remembers that this was the same accident he witnessed that morning long ago on his way to work. Then something he had almost forgotten about, that day on his way home he stopped at the accident scene, curious as the skid marks of the car and the burnt patch on the ground that were still visible. He remembers himself looking around and surveying the area and in looking down at the ground seeing something shiny, so he bent over to get a better look. In doing so he saw that, it was a necklace and picked it up. He remembers looking at it and that although the chain was broken, the charm was undamaged and remembers that it was a heart-shaped design with a diamond at its center. Finally he remembers getting into his truck and placing it in the ashtray, thinking that he would try to find out who it belongs to later but would dismiss it from his mind and had forgotten all about it.

Ryan focuses back on Albert. "If you don't mind me asking," Ryan says softly, "Do they have any hope she will ever recover?" Ryan Fighting with everything he has to remain calm, "It is not likely they say" Albert replies as his eyes fill with tears. "She is healthy other than the head trauma, they said we can only wait and see if she will ever wake up." Albert says, as a single tear runs down his face as he looks toward his wife.

"I am so sorry." Ryan says.

"Thank you."

"I will leave you alone now. It was nice meeting you."

"It was nice meeting you,"

Ryan begins to move away, and in doing so he is able to get a full view of the woman, but is still unable to see her face. In frustration Ryan scans the rest of the room looking for anything, a clue maybe. Without a thought his eyes go immediately to the embroidered sign over the bed and before he reads it, he knows what it says, "Love will find a way." It is at that moment all space and time has now stopped. He closes his eyes and knows the truth. Ryan takes a few steps and begins walking away, weak and dazed, he turns looking back at the husband and the room. Ryan pauses.

"Your wife!" Ryan blurts out.

Albert turns to Ryan, "I beg your pardon?"

"Your wife, I forgot to ask you what her name is."

"Sara, her name is Sara."

CHAPTER
EIGHT

It can't be, it couldn't be... Ryan looks toward the floor in front of him as it is coming in and out of focus; he feels dizzy, and the hallway is becoming narrower as he moves along to the point of feeling claustrophobic. Ryan falls heavily into a chair in the hallway, his legs weak and his breathing labored. He sits for a moment, perplexed, his hands shaking as they cover his face. The minutes are now feeling like hours as he tries desperately to understand what is happening. He looks toward the room; Albert is still standing in the doorway, staring into the heavens as if he was praying to God. Ryan begins to feel as if he needs to run into the room and look for himself. He is in denial but already knows it to be true. At the same time, he's thinking that this is crazy, it is not possible, and there is no way the lady in the room where Albert now stands is Sara.

Ryan struggles with himself, as the battle between reality and fantasy rage in his mind. Ryan musters the strength to stand; he pauses and looks again at Albert still standing in the doorway. He takes the few steps toward the nurses' station where one of the nurses who cared for him is standing. She turns toward Ryan, a surprised look of excitement on her face as she hugs Ryan.

"How are you?" she's asks.

"Fine, thank you for asking."

"What are you doing here?"

"Just visiting and saying thank you to everyone." with a notice-able strange look on his face.

"Are you all right?"

"I'm fine."

Ryan struggles to contain his emotions, the voice in his head badgering him to say something. Ryan pulls himself together long enough to ask, "The lady in the room, who is she?"

"Which lady?"

"Where the man is standing," Ryan replies.

"Who, Mrs. Adams?"

"*Adams…Sara Adams.* That is her husband, Albert, right?" Ryan asks already knowing the answer.

"Yes, that poor man. He is here every day."

Ryan looks down the hallway toward the room, "What do they say her chances are?" Ryan asks.

"Well, I am not supposed to discuss other patients but between you and me, not good," she replies. "She is in good health, but she may never come out of her coma."

"How old is she?" Ryan says not sure what else to ask.

The nurse hesitates, a strange look of why would he ask that question comes over her face. "She is young. I can't give you any specifics on a patient, but she is young."

"I understand," Ryan replies, "thank you."

"It was good seeing you." she says.

"It was good seeing you." Ryan replies, his mind focused on the room where Sara is. *Just beyond that doorway*, he thinks as he takes a few steps toward it.

As Ryan stands there, he notices that everything is so quiet even though he can see people moving around and can see their lips moving. It is silent. The faint sound of his own breathing and heartbeat begin to resonate through his body. He is paralyzed with all the thoughts and emotions coursing through his veins. He stands in the hallway for what feels like an eternity, his mind telling him that it is time to move, talk, do something, but he is unable to respond. There is nothing that can prepare you for the moment when all the things you have ever known or have come to believe make no sense and the unimaginable now is the new reality.

Finally Ryan comes back to reality, he feels the slight touch of someone passing him as he stands in the middle of the hallway. He is back in control of his senses, or somewhat anyway. He takes a breath and turns toward the exit. He pushes the elevator button, it is as if he can't leave. He knows it is Sara, but his logic overtakes him, and he enters the elevator once the doors open. What seems like a short walk to his truck has taken an eternity. He opens the truck door and gets in. As he sits there thinking and thinking, he keeps telling himself, this has to be the truth, while at the same time he is telling himself that this is not real, and that maybe, he thinks it was the accident and it caused him to imagine all this, he struggles to rationalize the situation but somewhere inside of him...He knows that is not the case.

Sara was in his life before that fateful day at the mill. Ryan thinks back to his conversation with Albert, he thinks about stopping that day at the accident site. His eyes turn toward the ashtray as he reaches down, he knows what is there but still can't bring himself to open it. With a shaking hand, he finds the courage to push open the ashtray and slowly sticks his hand inside, pulling out the necklace that he found on the road that day. He sits there as he raises the necklace to eye level and whispers, *this is how, this is how she found me.*

Ryan starts the truck and backs out of the parking spot; he stares at the hospital doors and then gazes up at the window where Sara lies. As the hospital fades from the view of the rearview mirror, he is gripped with anguish, fear, and disbelief. He is startled when the phone rings. He opens it and answers without looking at the caller ID. "Hello?" Ryan quickly realizes that it is Amber. "Hi, Babe." Amber says.

"Hello?" Ryan says again pretending to not be able to hear a response.

"Hello, Ryan…can you hear me?" Amber shouts, "Ryan!"

Ryan composes himself, looks at the phone and answers, "Yes, I'm here."

"Where are you?" Amber asks.

"On my way back from the hospital."

"Did you have nice visit?" Amber asks. Was everyone happy to see you?"

"Yes, it was good, and everyone was so nice," Ryan replies holding back every emotion consuming him. This, hand in hand with the struggle not to allow Amber to hear anything in his voice that could cause concern or raise questions.

"Oh, okay, that was nice." Amber replies. "How long before you're home?"

"I will be there in twenty minutes." Ryan replies and hangs up the phone without saying goodbye to Amber.

Ryan returns home and as he pulls into the driveway he is still shocked by all that has occurred. Ryan enters the house, Amber says, "Hi babe." Ryan makes his way to the couch without giving a response, Amber unaware of Ryan's present state, says, "Did anyone ask when you are coming back for more therapy?"

"Yes." Ryan replies, "But I told them I was not sure." As Ryan sits on the couch even Buddy, who was usually overjoyed, is calm, a strange stare on his face as Ryan looks down at him. It is as if he can see inside of him and has determined something is very wrong. Ryan makes his way into the house, Buddy trialing behind him, still calm and cautious. Amber is in the kitchen.

"Okay so tell me, how was your visit?" Amber asks.

"Fine." Ryan replies, "It was just a lot to see everyone." he says as he sits down at the kitchen table.

Amber turns with a towel in her hand and sees the troubled look on Ryan's face, "What?" she asks Ryan.

Ryan takes a moment to respond. "What?"

"Your face?" Amber says as she stands, staring at him.

"What is wrong with my face?" Ryan asks, annoyed.

"I know that face." Amber says, "What happened at the hospital?"

"Nothing."

"Okay, then what is wrong?"

"Why does something have to be wrong?"

Amber stares at Ryan, the frustration clearly showing on her face. "Okay, when you are ready to talk about whatever is bothering you, please come and talk to me." Amber states.

"There is nothing wrong. There is nothing to tell you, I am fine."

Amber turns toward back towards the counter, "Okay." She says as she looks down at the sink with a blank stare.

Ryan sits for a moment, thinking of what to do, what could he do? Ryan thinks to himself *I am not going to sit here, that's for sure* as he gets up from the table. Amber turns toward him but says nothing, the thoughts racing through her mind are apparent, but she just stares and continues drying the plate in her hand.

Ryan moves to the living room which serves as a makeshift office and sits at the desk. Buddy, now sitting at his side, his ears pinned back against his head, and is whimpering. Ryan reaches down and pats him on the head, Buddy's tail wags in hesitation. Ryan can feel that Buddy knows something is wrong and wonders for a moment if Buddy feels the stress and anxiety he is experiencing. He feels sorry for Buddy and tries to reassure him. "You okay boy?" Ryan says as he rubs his face, but Buddy seems reluctant to accept this gesture as reassuring.

Ryan turns his attention to the blank screen of the computer in front of him. He looks across the living room at Amber who is still drying dishes with her back turned toward him. Ryan moves the computer mouse around, and the computer begins its startup. Ryan types in the password, but the computer rejects it. Ryan dismisses the first attempt and tries again, and once again it is rejected. Ryan, in a loud voice, asks Amber, "Did you change the password?"

Amber turns "No, why?"

Ryan does not reply and tries again with yet a third rejection. Frustrated, he types it in again although this time checks to see what he has typed. As he looks at what he has typed Amber&Ryan01 should be what he is looking at, but instead he has typed "sara1201." He stares at the computer as if it was the one who got it wrong, then looks a second time just to make sure of what he was looking at. As he glances up, Amber is walking toward him to see what the problem is. Ryan quickly deletes his entry as Amber turns the monitor toward her.

Amber moves the keyboard toward her and types in the password which, of course, is accepted. Amber just looks at Ryan. "Thank you." Ryan says. Amber offers no reply as she walks back to the kitchen. A cold bead of sweat appears on his forehead as he watches Amber walk away. Ryan looks down at Buddy, even he can sense that it's a close call. He smiles at Buddy and starts typing and begins randomly looking at items on the internet. Ryan thinks to himself that if he looks like he is doing something, Amber would be less likely to want to talk to him about what happened at the hospital. As he clicks on the daily news and begins to read his mind is filled with the thoughts of what happened from his conversation with Albert to Sara, and finally the absurdity of everything that has happened to this point. On the screen Ryan sees the search bar; he dismisses the thought at that moment and decides to see what is happening outside of Grantsville. Ryan clicks on the link and begins to read about what is going on in the world. As he reads along, Amber walks back into the living room.

"What are your plans for the rest of the day?" she asks.

Ryan slowly gazes up from the screen and tells her, "Not much, I have to run a few errands later but nothing important, Why?"

"I was just wondering if we can finish our talk, now that you are better," Amber says.

The familiar feeling of dread comes over him, but he knows better than to let on that it's a problem. "Sure." Ryan replies and looks back down at the computer, Ryan is bewildered, *she is incredible,* he thinks, that conversation took place a long time ago and she acts like we talked about it yesterday.

Amber stands there for a moment staring at Ryan. As she begins walking away Amber says, "I'll get ready and come with you today when you run your errands, if that is okay."

"Sure, that would be nice." In his mind, he is thinking, *I know exactly what she is trying to do and wants.*

As Amber leaves the room, a light turns on in his mind, it is almost as if someone flipped a switch or what sounds like a voice in his head telling him to search. *Search…search for what?* He thinks.

He types keywords into the browser—near-death experience, after-life, coma—and presses enter. There on the screen is what amounts to a list of endless options, so he begins to filter through what has come up, most of what he clicks on seems like sensationalism, but as he focuses in on what he is reading and compares it to what he has experienced, he begins to see that many people have had similar or near-similar experiences. He is mesmerized at the similarity in these stories and the events that he has witnessed firsthand. *How can this all be?* he thinks.

As he scrolls through the volumes of information, he struggles to bring himself to believe in what amounts to ghost stories. Ryan continues to pour over the information then remembers the search bar on the previous page when he was looking at local news, *search,* he thinks, which gives him another idea; Ryan goes to that page and types in Sara, and hits enter with no results. He then types in Adams and hits enter with no results, nervously he looks across the living room for Amber, he feels like a teenage boy looking at a naughty magazine while looking for his mother, hoping not to get caught.

Then Ryan types in Sara Adams and at first nothing appears but links to dozens of people named Sara Adams. Ryan thinks and types in "Sara Adams, New Mexico." which yielded similar results. Ryan pauses and types "Sara Adams, New Mexico, coma," and hits enter, he stares in disbelief at the result, Ryan's body weakens by what he is reading in the header (Local Woman in a Coma—Sara Adams). He is hesitant and does not want to open the link, but his mind will not let him move on. His hand trembles as the mouse slides along the mouse pad, the indicator arrow slowly moving toward the posting, and in an instant, his finger, by sheer motor memory, clicks on the posting.

As Ryan begins to read he knows this is no longer a dream.

Sara Adams, age thirty-five, was involved in a serious automobile accident on December 1st, 2000 at 4:55 a.m. in the vicinity of Saw Mill Road and State Route 85, near mile marker 187. The victim, Sara Adams, was thrown from the vehicle, suffering severe head trauma and other minor injuries. She was transported by ambulance to Zuni Memorial Hospital, in Grantsville for medical treatment. A cause of the accident has not been determined.

Ryan is paralyzed; he can feel the tears in his eyes, as he reads the words to himself. Ryan abandons that posting and opens a subsequent post in which he reads that Sara Adams still remains in a coma eight months after her accident. Ryan looks up from the computer and is startled he is jerked into the moment as Amber is standing in front of him.

"What you are reading?"

Caught off guard, Ryan slowly tries to minimize the page. "Nothing." he replies, "Just sad stories on the Internet."

"Do you always cry when you read those things?"

"No."

"Then why are you crying now?" Amber asks as she giggles, trying to lighten the moment.

Ryan smiles at Amber, "I'm not."

"You always say that after you cry," Amber replies as she walks back toward the kitchen.

Ryan giggles so not to let on the emotional state he is facing right at that moment. As Amber walks away, Ryan opens the window and continues to read about Sara. He scrolls through the article, an image begins to appear in the article, and as he scrolls down, the image begins to come up, revealing itself with each second that Ryan is scrolling. The image moves to the center of the computer screen, any doubt that all this has been some sort of hallucination is laid to rest. The beautiful face staring back at him from the photograph in the article is the woman he met in his dream…Sara. The tears stream down his face, and he feels that he is losing consciousness. Ryan feels himself slipping off of the chair. The weight of his body becomes like jelly, and he is unable to right himself. Ryan is in the midst of a full panic attack and desperately trying to not pass out as he slumps in the chair.

Amber enters the room and immediately notices that something is wrong. "Ryan, what's wrong!" Amber screams and hurries toward him. Amber grabs Ryan by the shoulders as he collapses to the floor. "Ryan…Ryan, what is wrong? I'm going to call 911."

"No!" Ryan blurts out, "I'm fine…I'm fine, just give me a second."

Amber attempts to comfort Ryan who is now lying on the floor. As Ryan takes a moment to catch his breath, Amber looks up at the computer monitor and sees what Ryan was looking at. Amber has no idea who the woman is staring back at her from the computer screen is or could be? Amber looks down at Ryan. In her mind, she wants to ask Ryan who she is but based on what is happening, does not ask.

Amber's mind is racing, *What is wrong with Ryan? Who is the woman in the photo and what should I do?* All these thoughts fill her head as she looks down at Ryan. She can't help but think that the woman in the photo has something to do with what has just happened. Of course, at this point Amber sees no reason to believe that Ryan even knows who she is or that it had anything to do with what just happened, why would he?

Amber once again looks back at the photo. She doesn't understand it at that moment, but somewhere inside of her, she can feel that the photo means more to Ryan than just something he was reading about on the Internet and could possibly be the reason he is now laying on the ground. Amber dismisses all her thoughts and helps Ryan to his feet.

"Are you sure you're okay?" she asks.

"Yes, I'm fine." Ryan responds.

"Let me help you to the couch." Amber says placing his arm around her neck and on her shoulder.

As they make their way to the couch, Ryan looks back one last time at the monitor which was slightly turned toward the living room when he fell. He sees Sara looking back at him as Amber is helping him to the couch. Ryan turns his head back toward the living room, and sees that Amber is staring at him. It is as if she knows what he was doing. Amber's eyes fill with tears as she is now certain that all of this is connected and that Ryan is holding a secret. Amber continues to help Ryan onto the couch. Once there Amber stands in front of him saying nothing. It is at that moment Ryan realizes that he can no longer keep this secret to himself and is left saying to himself, *What do I do now…what do I do now?*

CHAPTER
NINE

Ryan awakens to the familiar feel of his own bed beneath him. He stares up at the popcorn ceiling and thinks back to his childhood when he would imagine the small glitter flakes were stars and how he dreamed of traveling among them. The sound of movement interrupts his daydreaming, and his eyes track toward the source of the sound. Amber is standing in the doorway. Ryan pauses and takes a breath, clearing the lump in his throat as both of them play the who-will-talk-first scenario.

Amber breaks the silence and in a soft voice asks, "You okay?"

Ryan stares at the ceiling, replying, "Yeah, I'm fine." He avoids making eye contact and can make out Amber's silhouette using his peripheral vision but still unwilling to turn his head toward her and engage her directly.

Amber is still standing in the doorway, her hands nervously rubbing together, it is her body's way of attempting to relieve the nervous energy that she is experiencing. "Can I get you anything?" Amber asks.

"No, I'm fine."

Amber continues to stand in the doorway. He senses that she is not going to simply walk away or somehow let the events of the night before fade from her memory. Reluctantly Ryan turns toward Amber, their eyes connect, and Amber begins to tear up. Ryan quickly looks away, staring back at the ceiling. "I'm fine, Amber!" Ryan blurts out. He can feel and see Amber move toward him.

"Are you fine?"

"Yes." Ryan replies and turns his body away from Amber, clutching the pillow and staring at the distant wall. He can sense that Amber is moving closer, he can feel that she is now at the edge of the bed. Her stare is felt by Ryan even though he has still not turned toward her.

She reaches out and touches the blanket where Ryan's leg rest beneath. Ryan pulls away ever so slightly, in a move that was almost visibly unnoticeable but yet felt by Amber. Amber pulls her hand away quickly, the pain in her heart almost visible to the naked eye.

Amber is undeterred and continues to stand at the edge of the bed. Ryan relents to Amber's persistence and turns toward her, sitting up in the bed. They stare at each other for what feels like an eternity. Ryan feels for Amber and can sense the pain in her heart as well as see it in her eyes.

"What do you want from me Amber?" he asks Amber, wanting it to be over.

"I want to know if you are okay, Ryan?—I think you need to go to the doctor."

Ryan is somewhat relieved because it appears that she is more concerned for medical reasons and not the reason he was expecting. "I am fine; I don't need to go to the doctor!"

"I know you feel fine now, but we need to make sure there is nothing else going on." Amber says.

"Nothing else is going on." Ryan replies but knows that she is not going to give up, as she slowly walks toward the doorway, staring back at him with reluctance. Trying to avoid any additional conflict Ryan breaks the silence and says, "Okay, let me get ready and we can go."

Amber turns and begins to walk toward the door, telling Ryan, "I will make you something to eat."

He does not reply and moves to the edge of the bed, his elbows resting on his knees and his hands clutching his face. As he sits there, he can hear Amber on the telephone making the appointment and telling whomever she is talking to what had happened. Ryan steps into the shower, a small token of silence with nothing but the sound of the running water; his mind is given a break from the thoughts barreling through it. As he gets out of the shower and begins drying his hair, he finds himself staring at his own distorted reflection in the mirror. Ryan swipes his hand across the mirror and removes the steam, although the image is sharper, the reflection he sees is still distorted. Ryan can barely recognize the person staring back at him. He continues to get ready and can hear Amber moving about in the kitchen.

As Ryan makes his way out of the bedroom, he can see that she is cooking; his guilt is looming as he knows that she is a good wife and a good person, yet all he can think of is Sara. He pulls a chair and sits at the kitchen table, resting his cane against the other chair. Amber brings him a plate, nothing fancy, just a few eggs and a few strips of bacon. *Not real bacon of course*, he thinks to himself. *Turkey bacon…it tastes like cardboard*, Ryan thinks as he says thank you.

Amber turns away and does not say anything as she looks at the facial expression of Ryan looking at the plate almost like a child who has been given a plate of vegetables to eat. Amber brings him a small glass of orange juice before sitting across the table from him. There is an ominous silence in the kitchen; it almost feels as if it is one of those silent moments that should not be broken, so they both sit quietly, neither willing to say anything even though they would like to. Ryan makes every effort not to make eye contact, but he can feel Amber's stare.

Amber finally gives in and asks, "Would you like anything else?"

Ryan just shakes his head and softly says, "No, I'm fine."

Amber continues to stare at Ryan and without warning and wasting no more time asks, "Do you know that person?"

Ryan gasps, inside he is trying to fight every instinct not to react to her question. "What person?" he asks, knowing full well what it is she is asking about.

As Ryan looks up, Amber says, "The lady you were looking at on the computer?"

"No, not really."

"No, not really?"…"What does that mean, no, not really?" Amber asks, gazing at Ryan.

"No, not really." Ryan replies again.

"Okay, what does that mean, no, not really?"

Ryan, not having a good answer, replies, "I was just looking."

"At what, Ryan?" Amber ask in a loud tone, Ryan sensing that she was not satisfied with his response, says, "Someone at the hospital told me that the lady in the photograph was involved in a car accident and was in the same hospital as me, that's all. I was just curious to see who it was."

"Okay, why would you be curious?"

Ryan snaps back in a loud voice as he slams the fork forcibly on the table. "I was curious, can I not be curious?"

Amber is stunned by his reaction and is unsure what to say or do.

Ryan regains his composure and apologizes for the outburst. "I was just curious because that lady is in a coma on the same floor I was on." Amber listens intently. "So the day I went to the hospital I met her husband."

"You met her husband? Why would you meet her husband?" Amber asks, Ryan does not reply.

"What is her name?" Amber asks.

Ryan looks down at the table, unable to bring himself to make eye contact with Amber. "Sara," he mutters as he gets up from that table. "Can we go now?"

Amber remembers hearing that name before. She searches her memory for that information, her thoughts racing as she pretends to be unalarmed by Ryan's answers in response to her question. *It is time to go*, Ryan thinks as they make their way to the truck.

Ryan holds open the door for Amber, and they set off to go the hospital. Ryan knows that there is nothing medically wrong with him and there is no doctor there that can cure him of what is really troubling him but he is willing to do anything that would not cause any further conflict with Amber. The drive is quiet. Amber stares out the window, watching the passing telephone poles as they speed by. Ryan is hesitant to start a conversation, afraid of what she may ask, afraid of what he might say. What Ryan doesn't realize is at that same moment, Amber is thinking the same thing while being haunted by the name Sara, *Where have I heard that name it before*, she thinks. Her frustration grows and grows as she is unable to make her mind release the information that she is desperately searching for.

As they pull up to the hospital, Amber wipes a tear from her eye without letting Ryan see. She watches as Ryan gets out of the truck and walks around to open her door. Amber senses that Ryan seems nervous, but yet excited to be there. She continues to try to make sense of what she is feeling, all the while arguing with her own mind, demanding the information regarding the name Sara. As they walk inside, Amber is greeted by some of the medical staff that took care of Ryan after his accident. The staff then turn to Ryan who is cordial but distracted. Amber tugs at Ryan's shirt in an effort to get him to focus on what is taking place right in front of him but can see that Ryan's focus is elsewhere. Amber begins looking in the direction of what is distracting Ryan and yanks at Ryan's shirt, sharply drawing his attention and breaking his distraction.

"They are talking to you." Amber tells Ryan.

"I know." Ryan replies as he turns toward the staff, a smile comes to his face but it is a smile of insincerity.

As they wait in the hallway to see the doctor, Ryan's leg nervously shakes and is once again distracted with something down the hallway. Amber says nothing and continues to go through her memory for the name Sara. Suddenly Ryan can hear a distant voice calling his name; and for a brief moment he thinks that it may be Sara who is calling him and quickly looks up. His hopes fade as another yank of his shirt by Amber snaps his attention to the person actually calling his name. He reluctantly gets out of his chair and approaches the nurse who is calling out for him. "Ryan," the nurse calls out again, he nods his head yes and begins to follow the nurse through the door. As Ryan follows the nurse down the small hallway, they finally make their way into the small examination room. The nurse tells Ryan to go ahead and have a seat on the table and the doctor will be right with you, "Thank you," Ryan replies, and slowly steps up to the table and lifts himself onto it. Ryan sits in silence for a few minutes and the door opens. And a man in a white lab coat enters the room, "Hello, Ryan."—"I am Dr. Myers,"

"Nice to meet you, doc." Ryan replies.

"How are you feeling today?"

"Fine."

"I understand you fainted last night."

"It's probably nothing."

"Nothing, huh?" the doctor comments, a look of disbelief mixed with concern on his face, "Go ahead and scoot all the way onto the table and let me take a look at you," the doctor says, Ryan moves his butt further onto the examination table, causing the loud crumpling sound of the white paper as he tries to get situated. Amber who followed Ryan into the room quietly sits on a small stool next to the table.

"Are you feeling dizzy or light headed today?" The doctor asks, placing a stethoscope on Ryan's chest.

"No."

"Okay, take a deep breath for me and let it out." the doctor instructs Ryan.

Ryan takes in a large gasp of air. The doctor moves the stethoscope, and again, Ryan takes in another breath of air and exhales. The doctor moves the stethoscope.

"And one more time—Well everything sounds fine, go ahead and lay back," the doctor says, Ryan lays down while he presses on his stomach and after a few pushes the doctor says, "Okay, go ahead and sit up." Ryan sits up and watches as the doctor makes a few notes on his chart but is unable to read them. "We should get some blood work while you are here just to make sure we are not missing anything." he tells Ryan, "So hang out here for a minute and let me get that order started."

"Thank you, doc," Ryan says and as he walks toward the door, Ryan asks, "Hey doc, the lady in the coma Sara, how is she doing?"

The doctor turns and looks at Ryan then at Amber. Amber abruptly turns to Ryan a blank stare on her face as she stands there, she no doubtingly has the same question in her mind the doctor had, *why would he ask that question?*

"As good as can be expected, I guess." he replies, as he turns and leaves the room.

Amber continues to stare at Ryan. Ryan can feel the weight of her stare but is unwilling to engage her. The awkward silence is broken by the phlebotomist who has entered the room to draw Ryan's blood. "Hello, I am going to be taking some blood from you now." The young lady states as she ties an elastic truncate around Ryan's arm and inserts the needle. The pain of the needle takes Ryan back to the cottage and Sara. No words are spoken as the small stream of blood fills the vials, but Ryan can still see Amber staring at him through the corner of his eye. The doctor returns to the room as Ryan rolls down his sleeve and steps off the examination table.

The doctor tells Ryan, "We should have the results in a few days, once the results come in we will give you a call... Before I let you go." Ryan pauses and turns toward the doctor, Amber stands up and moves next to Ryan. "I was looking at your chart that you were conditionally released to return to work some time ago? How is that going?" Ryan looks at Amber then back at the doctor, "I have had some vacation time I have been using so I have not been back yet." Ryan replies. Amber looks at Ryan knowing that because he has been so preoccupied with things he is keeping to himself, he has not wanted to go back to work and had little to do with using up vacation time. "Oh." the doctor replies, as he looks at Ryan's chart, "I also see that you were referred for physical therapy after your release from the hospital, have you completed that?" Ryan looks at Amber again, then back at the doctor, "No, I have been doing it on my own at the house." Amber looks on knowing that he has not. "Okay." the doctor says, "Is there anything else going on that could have caused you to faint?" the doctor asks. Ryan stares for a moment then shakes his head "No, everything has been good." Amber is doing everything she can to remain calm and quiet. "Okay." the doctor says, "Like I said we will give you a call when your results come back."

"Thank you Doc." Ryan says and makes his way toward the door with Amber following closely behind.

As the two walk down the hallway, the sounds of the nursing staff is muffled by Ryan's thoughts of Sara who is only feet away. He is desperately fighting the feelings and urges to go to her all the while appearing normal, as normal as he can for Amber's sake. Ryan is finding it harder and harder to walk away, he feels as if someone is turning up the gravity specifically for him, making it harder and harder to lift every step. As they exit the building, Amber takes the lead. He can see that she is visibly upset. Ryan once again opens the truck door for her, Amber quickly gets in, grabs the door handle and abruptly closes the door before Ryan has a chance to close it. Ryan stands silent for a minute before walking around the truck and gets in. The silence is ominous, He places the key into the ignition and thinks how strange it is that he can actually hear the clicking sound of the key as it passes over the tumblers. Amber turns to Ryan, stares, but says nothing. Ryan looks back with the same response. *The drive home is going to be a long one*, Ryan thinks.

Amber is consumed with mixed feelings of anger, love and sorrow when suddenly it hits her! She turns to Ryan. "You do know her."

"Who?"

"Sara."

"What are you talking about?"

"The day you woke up from your coma, you called out her name."

"You're crazy."

Amber wants so much to believe that none of this is real, but in her soul she knows that it is true. "Don't tell me I'm crazy Ryan, I see it on your face."

Ryan thinks for a second, his mind turns to a thought of his mother who would always say "What's wrong with your face?" She could always tell when he was hiding something or something was wrong. He knows it is now or never but decides to lie. How can he tell her the truth? How could he explain what really happened?

"I must have heard her name at some point while I was in the hospital then with the accident got everything all mixed up."

"Stop lying to me, Ryan, were you seeing her?" Amber shouts.

"How could I see her?...She is in a coma!"

"Before the accident Ryan. You know what I am talking about," Amber says, "before the accident that left her like that."

"No," Ryan replies. "I was not seeing her."

"Then what, Ryan?...Tell me, then what!" Amber shouts.

Ryan takes a deep breath and no longer wants to continue the game that they are playing. He pulls the truck off to the side of the road and stares at the windshield. He knows he must tell her the truth no matter how unbelievable or impossible it sounds. Ryan takes another deep breath and turns toward Amber who is now facing him, her cheeks covered in tears.

"I had a dream about her."

"A dream about her? What you are talking about Ryan?"

The minutes, then what seems like hours tick by as Ryan begins to tell Amber all that has happened. Ryan thinks to himself, *If I'm going to tell her, then I'm going to tell her everything.* As Ryan lays out the events that transpired, Ryan can see that Amber is going from sadness to anger as he continues to tell his tale. She abruptly stops Ryan almost to the completion of his story.

"Stop Ryan! Why are you doing this?" Amber asks, "This entire story is ridiculous Ryan…seriously!" she screams.

"It's true, Amber," Ryan proclaims. "Why would I make all this up? It's what happened,"

"I don't think we need to talk about it anymore!" Amber shouts, "If you can't be honest, fine! But I am not going to sit here and let you make a fool of me!" Amber angrily replies as she turns toward the window and continues crying.

Why is all this happening? Ryan thinks. "Why is this all happening to me?" Ryan says out loud.

"Just take me home." Amber whispers.

"Please, Amber." Ryan pleads, "You have to believe me."

"Just take me home," Amber mutters, the sound of sadness in her voice is paralyzing.

Ryan starts the truck and pulls back onto the road. Amber continues to sob. He wants to console her, he wants to bring her comfort but knows that is impossible. *How can I comfort her with a truth that is so unbelievable?* Ryan thinks, *what have I done? More importantly, how can I now undo what I have told her and how do I now make right an affair I've had even if it was only in a dream? Most importantly, how can I now live with the fact that I must stop loving what amounts to a figment of my imagination, in order to save the love I have in reality?*

As they pull into the driveway, Amber begins to open the door of the truck before the truck has even come to a stop, and tries to get out. "Stop!" Amber yells. "Stop the truck!" She shouts.

Ryan presses hard on the brake as the truck slides to a stop causing the sound of gravel being drug on the ground. Amber leaps out of the truck and runs toward the house. Ryan slowly gets out as Buddy runs to greet him, he kneels down and vigorously rubs Buddy as he is panting, and wagging his tail, but it brings him little comfort today. Ryan makes his way to the front porch when he hears the slamming of the bedroom door and decides not to go in. He takes refuge on the porch swing, Buddy at his side as Ryan stares out onto the yard and is unable to believe all that has happened.

I am not sure how to go on, he thinks. I am so torn between the woman I have loved my whole life and a woman in my dreams. How can all this be happening? Ryan turns toward the door. He knows that he must enter and try to make this right for Amber, but as he grips the door handle, he thinks of Sara. *I love her...I miss her...* He shakes his head, and opens the door. As he stands there in the darkness only one thought comes to his mind, given the choice between the real world and the world he shared with Sara, what world would he choose?

CHAPTER

TEN

The weight of Ryan's situation and circumstances has begun to take its toll. As hard as Ryan tries, he cannot escape the pain, sadness, and destitute that he feels at this moment. Ryan finds himself lying on the bed as he has done hundreds of times before; however, this time would be very different. He is struggling to gain the strength to even get out of bed. His body feels as if someone has literally taken out his very spirit and replaced it with a heavy wet blanket; every movement Ryan attempts is an effort of futility, its soggy enveloping grasp holds him firmly in place. As he turns his head he can see Amber is lying next to him. He wants to say something, try to explain, but the mere thought of the energy it would take discourages him. Ryan looks away slowly and through the corner of his eye, he can see Amber staring up at the ceiling; her stare is so focused and intense Ryan can only imagine the thoughts that are going through her mind but knows he dare not ask what they are. Amber abruptly gets up and goes into the bathroom. She usually said good morning but that would not be the case this morning. He can hear the familiar sounds of the shower and knows that he can take a moment to gather his thoughts before she emerges.

Ryan finds himself in a fierce debate with himself as to whether he should get out of bed, then hears the shower turn off and takes a breath, knowing that his time is short. As he continues to struggle, the bathroom door opens slightly.

Amber peers through the partially open door, "Are you getting up today?"

"Yes, I am getting up." Ryan replies as he turns onto his side, away from Amber's stare. He can hear the door open wider.

Amber steps into the doorway, a towel wrapped around her, still dripping wet from her shower. "You need to get up." She says in a raised tone.

"I don't feel good."

There is a hesitation and an awkward silence as he can feel Amber still standing in the doorway. The awkward silence is broken when the bathroom door closes, to Ryan's relief. Amber has chosen not to pursue this any further. She finishes getting ready and walks out of the bedroom. She makes no attempt to engage Ryan and does not even turn toward him as she leaves the room. Ryan has now been in bed the entire day; Amber has made no attempt to check on him even though he has heard her moving in and out of the house all day. Ryan knows he has no right but feels angry that Amber is being indifferent to him, but at the same time can see why, *How can I be angry?* he thinks to himself. As he is completing that thought, the bedroom door opens.

"Are you just going to stay in bed all day?" Amber asks in a condescending voice.

"I don't feel good I said." Ryan replies in an angered tone.

"What is wrong with you?…Your stomach, head, what?"

"I just don't feel good, is that okay?"

Amber stands in the doorway; Ryan makes no effort to make eye contact. "Are we going to talk about all this? Are you ready to tell me what is really going on? …and this time the truth" she says her hands shaking along with her voice, trying desperately not to cry.

"I told you what is going on. What else do you want me to tell you?"

"The truth, Ryan…the truth!"

"I am telling you the truth!"

Amber stands and stares not saying another word, before slamming the bedroom door. Ryan can hear her heavy footsteps, as she makes her way across the living room. The sound of the front door slamming startles him, and even though he knows he should go after her he decides to stay right where he is. As Ryan hears Amber getting into her car and driving away, he knows he must try to make things right but in the back of his mind he knows that he has neither the strength nor the will to even try.

The sun is now setting as Ryan gazes out the window watching the last few minutes of daylight fade to darkness. Amber is still not home. Ryan thinks he is concerned, but the feeling of sadness for not being with Sara outweighs any concern for Amber right now. Although he knows he needs to pull himself together and try to repair his situation with Amber, he is completely consumed with the images of Sara in his mind, the tears welling up in his eyes as he sits up and moves to the edge of the bed. With all the strength he can muster, he stands and makes his way to the kitchen.

The house is so cold, dark, and quiet. He can see Buddy in the twilight lying on his doggy bed but is perplexed as to why Buddy has not made an effort to come to him. It is as if he is scared to move, his tail wagging slightly his ears are lying flat against his head. Ryan opens the refrigerator, and looks inside, the light from the refrigerator illuminating the kitchen. As he gazes looking for something to eat, he glances to the kitchen counter where he can see there is a bottle of vodka. Ryan stares at the bottle, hesitates, then closes the refrigerator door and makes his way to it. Ryan holds up the bottle and looks at it, no real thought in his mind, just a strange feeling. He opens the cabinet and retrieves a small rock glass, blowing into it.

Ryan pulls out a chair from the kitchen table and sits down the bottle of vodka and rock glass in the other hand. He opens the bottle with one hand, spinning the cap onto the table. He pours himself a drink and holds up the glass to the small amount of light left in the room. *I am not a drinker,* he thinks to himself, as he draws the glass to his lips. Ryan has always held firm that drinking was never a good thing. His father was a drinker along with his brother, and through the years their indulgence in this poison never had a good or happy outcome. Ryan's thoughts go back to a time when his father abused his mother with the help of alcohol, the nights he cowered on the floor crying, the image of his father standing over his mother shouting and cursing at her as she begged him to stop. His father was a good man, but the mix of his own demons and alcohol always morphed him into an unrecognizable entity that Ryan vowed he would never become.

As the alcohol passes through his mouth and down his throat, the burn of its power causes him to squint his eyes. At that moment he realizes that this small action would be leading him down a dark path, a path to which the destination may not be a place he would like or hope to be. With that thought, he pours himself another and another until the night begins to fade away.

The light of a new day awakens him; Ryan slowly opens his eyes and picks his head off of the table where he is still sitting in his underwear. On the kitchen table, Ryan sees the empty bottle of vodka lying on its side, proof of what he has done. Ryan looks around the room, his head throbbing from the alcohol. He takes a moment to listen for any movement from Amber, but there is only silence. As Ryan attempts to make his way to the bedroom he notices that Amber is sleeping on the couch. She looks so peaceful, and his heart hurts thinking of what she must be feeling and what she is obviously going through, yet his thought is only temporary as the dread of not being able to see Sara and the pain of missing her overtakes him.

Ryan makes his way to the bathroom, bumping into the wall and doorway on his journey there, then notices that he is still drunk and balance would not be in the cards this morning. As he sways in front of the toilet, he sees that this would not have been the first time he has urinated lately; the evidence on his underwear is unmistakable that he did not make it to the bathroom the last time he had to go. Ryan steps out of the bathroom and collapses onto the bed, completely aware he is still wearing his urine-soaked underwear. As he lays there, Amber comes to the bedroom. She stands just inside the doorway saying nothing.

"What?" Ryan whispers.

"What?" Amber whispers back. "Is that all you have to say?... What is going on with you?" "Nothing is wrong." Ryan replies. "Obviously, there is something very wrong."

"I just had a few drinks, so what?"

"A few." Amber replies in a condescending voice.

"Yes, a few god dammit." Ryan answers, as he looks at Amber with contempt.

"You know what, Ryan, I love you! And you are acting like you don't care. Why are you drinking? What is going on with you? ... Talk to me... Why won't you talk to me?" Amber says in a shaky voice.

"Enough, Amber…enough," Ryan replies, as he sits up and tries to maintain his composure. The pounding of his head and her relentless verbal assault is excruciating.

Try as Ryan might the next several days would be a repeat of today's events. Ryan has managed to create for himself a version of Ground Hog Day of which he finds himself unable to escape. What started out as a way to ease the pain he was feeling has turned into something he swore he would never become (His father)… Ryan stares up at the ceiling and wonders if this is how it began for him. *What am I doing?* he thinks. Unknowingly to Ryan, Amber has contacted the mine and explained to them, without stating the obvious, that Ryan was in no condition to return to work. She felt the accident was not only responsible for Ryan's physical state but also for his mental state as well, and why he had not been back to work after being cleared by the doctor. Amber, desperate and out of ideas she has also contacted the doctor, to see what if anything he could do to help Ryan. With no other explanation for what is happening Amber is convinced that the accident and specifically the head injury is the root cause which would explain his mood change, drinking, and the crazy story he told her several days ago.

Ryan looks up from the floor, a familiar view over the last several days as his relationship with alcohol has left him with no other choice but to sleep on the floor. From this vantage point he can see the legs of Amber standing over him. Without saying a word, Amber helps him to the couch. Ryan manages to slur "Thank you." He finds himself thinking, *What am I doing? What is wrong with me?* He looks to Amber and says, "I'm going to be late for work... I need to get back to work." Ryan says, almost saying he has to get back to Sara.

"No you don't," Amber replies, knowing that Ryan had not been back to work since the accident. "We need to focus on getting you better."

"Better," Ryan replies, "better than what?" Ryan slurs as he tries to right himself on the couch.

"You let me worry about that." Amber replies. "I need you to get up and get ready."

"Ready for what?"

"You have a doctor's appointment today."

"No, I don't."

"Just get ready, please."

After several more minutes of struggle Amber manages to get Ryan ready and has helped him to the truck. Little is said on their way to the hospital. Ryan's thoughts are only for the sadness that he feels missing Sara. Amber helps Ryan out of the truck and into the hospital doors, he notices that the same people who cared for him when his accident happened are now looking at him with a look of sadness or even pity. He feels ashamed but at the same time anger. *What right do they have to judge me?* he thinks.

The usual walk to the doctor has taken a different path this morning and into a wing of the hospital that he has not been in before. "Where are we going?" Ryan asks.

"To see the doctor," Amber replies. Amber sits Ryan in a small waiting room as she walks to the desk to check him in. Amber returns to where Ryan is sitting and begins to fill out forms given to her by the receptionist.

"What are we doing here?" Ryan asks.

"Seeing the doctor, I told you that already."

"What doctor?…Why are we here?" Ryan asks again as he begins to get agitated and wants to stand up and leave.

Amber clutches his hand. "Ryan, please, just stay still for a minute, for me, please." Amber pleads.

To Ambers relief the wait is short *unusual for the typical doctor visit*, she thinks as Ryan's name is called out by the young lady who has come to the door. Ryan has sobered up slightly and can see that the person who came to the door and called his name is not a nurse but instead is a young woman in a pantsuit, his mind desperately trying to make sense of it all. The lady says nothing to Ryan and leads him down a short hallway and opens a door at the end of it.

"What's going on?" Ryan asks.

"I'll explain in a minute, Ryan."

Ryan realizes that the room they have entered is not an examination room, and as Ryan scans the room, he can see and now understands what type of doctor this young lady is. "Please, sit down." The young lady tells Ryan.

Ryan, now agitated, shouts "I don't want to sit down!—Why am I here?"

"Please, sit down, and I will explain what is happening."

Ryan reluctantly sits, his eyes continuing to scan the room.

"I am Dr. Fisher," she says, "And I am a psychologist."

"I am not crazy!" Ryan blurts out.

"No one said you were…Do you think you are crazy?" she asks.

Ryan pauses and thinks to himself, *I have watched enough crime shows, like* Law and Order *to know that this is how they talk to people whom are considered to have mental or emotional issues.* "No, I don't think I'm crazy." Ryan says.

"Okay, so can you tell me what's going on?"

"Going on with what?"

"I understand that you are having some trouble."

"Who told you that? I'm fine."

"Okay, then tell me why you think you are here?"

"I have been drinking the last several days, so what?" Ryan says.

"Over the last several days, is this something you normally do?"

"No, I don't really drink." Ryan replies, "And yes over the last several days." Ryan says in a sarcastic tone.

"Okay, can you tell me why the last several days?"

"I just felt like it."

"Okay, is there something troubling you?" The doctor asks, pauses and before Ryan can answer asks, "I understand you have been experiencing hallucinations. Is that the reason?"

"Who is telling you all this. Is it Amber?"

"Are you having hallucinations?" she asks again.

Ryan sits back in the chair, a look of fatigue on his face. *I can't do this anymore,* he thinks. Ryan pauses, takes a deep breath and reluctantly says, "I am not sure. I don't think it is a hallucination."

"Okay, can you tell me what you think they are?" she asks.

"I…I have had several dreams of a woman." Ryan says as he looks toward the ground.

"Other than your wife?"

"Yes."

"Okay, can you tell me more about it?" the doctor asks as Ryan struggles.

He knows what she will think if he tells her the truth. *But what if she can help?* he thinks. *What do I have to lose?* he thinks and begins to tell her the story. He watches as the doctor listens intensely, writing on a notepad between glances. Suddenly a feeling of absolute fear comes over him, his hand trembles as he realizes that what he is saying and admitting to will not have a positive outcome. The paranoia inside of him is growing.

"Do you love this woman?… The woman in your dreams?" the doctor asks, Ryan can hear her ask the question but her voice sounds different as if she is in a long tunnel.

"What?" Ryan asks, as he incoherently stares.

"I asked if you loved this woman, do you love her?" the doctor's voice is now even further away although he can still see her sitting in front of him.

Ryan suddenly jumps to his feet and shouts, "I have to get out of here…let me out of here!"

"Ryan. I need you to calm down." she says in a calm voice.

However Ryan is now becoming more and more agitated as the seconds pass.

In a calm tone she says again "Calm down, Ryan …I need you to calm down."

Ryan continues to shout and is now trying to get to the door to leave. Grabbing a hold of the door handle, he can hear the doctor shouting "Orderlies…orderlies!" as Ryan gets the door open.

He feels a sudden impact of something which knocks him to the ground and realizes it is the orderly that the doctor was calling out to. Ryan struggles as the momentum carries them into the waiting room, knocking over chairs and tipping over a table.

Ryan begins to scream, "Amber…Amber! Help me…help me." Then without thought, he begins to blurt out, "Sara…Sara…" He realizes what he said and begins to say, "No…no…no…help me, please, help me?"

The orderly manages to wrestle Ryan onto his stomach. He can see Amber, her eyes filled with tears as she is ushered away while he is being restrained by the orderlies. From his position on the floor,

Ryan can see the bottom of the pantsuit of the doctor and hear her say, "Let's get him to a room. We are going to sedate him."

Ryan struggles and screams as another orderly has come to assist, and with his help Ryan is subdued. He knows the fight is over as he can feel the sting of the needle going into his arm, a warm sensation comes over him then everything goes dark.

Ryan's eyes open. He finds himself restrained to what amounts to be a flat metal table. He is groggy from the sedation but can hear the people in the room. In the midst of all the voices he can hear a familiar voice. *Amber,* he thinks. He wants to call out to her, but the medication they gave him has left him in a fog. After all that has happened, he realizes his fate as he can hear the doctor tell Amber that he was going to be checked into the hospital for his own safety and the safety of others.

Ryan turn his eyes to the ceiling and thinks, *I have spent a lifetime committed to my wife, job, and family without regret. But I know, this moment will be the one moment I will regret rest of my life. How will I survive this?...Sara where are you?*

CHAPTER
ELEVEN

Ryan is once again staring up at the ceiling but fears that he will not be looking at the popcorn ceiling of his home anytime soon. He can feel the tug of restraints on his wrist and ankles; the fuzzy feel of the restraints are strangely comfortable but of course confining. As he fidgets, it is not the restraints on his wrists and ankles that are the source of his panic, it is the leather strap that is cinched across his chest that is the most disturbing. Ryan strains and thinks maybe it is not the most ideal situation for someone who suffers from claustrophobia to be strapped down like this. The growing mania inside of him is as real as the restraints that bind him. Ryan can feel himself sliding into that panic. Totally immobilized, mentally, spiritually, and now physically, his eyes scan the ceiling as he thinks that this is not something he envisioned he would ever see in his lifetime.

As he struggles against the bindings, he hears the door open. Ryan moves his head from left to right to see who has come into the room, his line of sight diminished by the restraints, unable to see anyone. "Who's there!" he shouts. Whomever the person or persons now in the room remain silent. "Who's there?" Ryan shouts again.

His eyes are moving widely around at the limited view of his surroundings. Suddenly a voice said, "Hello Ryan."

Sara, Ryan thinks but his hope is quickly diminished as he hears, "Hello, Ryan. It is Dr. Fisher."

"How are you feeling today?"

"Please, what is happening, Please?"

"It's okay Ryan." the doctor replies. "You need to remain calm, and I will do my best to help you.—Can you tell me how you are feeling?" she asks again.

"How do you think I am feeling? I'm tied to a bed."

"I'm sorry about that, but it was necessary."

"Why are you doing this to me?… I want to go home."

"I can't do that."

Ryan begins to become more and more despondent as the seconds tick by and begins to say "I want to go home." over and over again.

"Please, calm down, I am only here to help you."

Ryan is breaking from reality and continues to repeat himself over and over again, "I want to go home...I want to go home."

As the doctor continues to try and persuade Ryan to calm down Ryan begins to struggle widely and begins to scream, and without thought, his screams turn to saying, "Sara...Sara...Sara..."

Dr. Fisher quickly exits the room as Ryan continues to scream. Suddenly the door opens again. Ryan can hear that it is more than one person this time that has entered the room. Ryan feels the stern grasp of someone on his arm and then a cold wet sensation at the crook of his arm, Ryan looks up at the ceiling, he knows what is coming next as the needle penetrates his arm. Ryan turns to the side of the injection and pleads, "No...no...no...please...no."

As the sedation begins to take hold, the euphoric numbness of his senses dull as his thoughts turn to Sara. *Where are you...where are you?* he mumbles to himself as he slowly loses consciousness.

Ryan awakens from his most recent run in with his captors, and is tormented that he is still restrained to the table. Ryan takes a moment and gathers his thoughts. He knows that he must try to remain calm and still if he has any hopes of getting out of the restraints. As he formulates a plan to comply, the door opens. Ryan takes a deep breath and remains silent. He can hear the footsteps as they approach. He sees Dr. Fisher as she stands looking over at him.

"How you are doing?"

Ryan, staying true to his plan, replies, "Better, thank you."

"You seem better."

"Yes, I am much better." Ryan replies, trying not to press the issue and offers no request to remove the restraints of course.

Ryan can feel the doctor as she stands there for a moment staring at him then asks, "Do you think you can remain calm long enough to have these restraints removed?"

Ryan turns toward the doctor, "Yes, I will be fine, I promise."

Dr. Fisher stares at Ryan for a moment longer as if she is studying his eyes, looking for any hint of defiance. Ryan makes as little eye contact as possible, the sweat beading on his forehead. Dr. Fisher looks away from Ryan and toward the door, and hears her call for the orderly. The door opens, he can hear several footsteps enter the room. Holding true to his plan, he makes no sudden movements nor offers any eye contact as the orderlies remove the restraints.

In the meantime Ryan can hear Dr. Fisher is talking. He can hear her voice and understands what she is saying, but between his relief that the restraints are being removed and thoughts of Sara, her words have little meaning. "Can you sit up for me?" she asks.

Ryan lifts himself and sits on the edge of the table. He watches as the doctor grabs the small stool, rolls it toward him, and sits down. As she settles onto the stool, Ryan draws his attention to the doctor but can see through the small window of the door that the orderlies have not gone far and appear eagerly awaiting their call to arms. Ryan continues telling himself, *You need to make no sudden moments or utter any loud outburst causing them to react.* Ryan looks down at the floor, rubbing his wrist where the restraints left their impressions.

"I want to talk to you about why we are here today, is that okay?" the doctor asks.

"Okay." Ryan replies softly.

"I need you to tell me about the dreams you are having…Are you still having them and if you are, can you talk about that?…Will that be okay?"

Ryan just nods and continues to stare at the floor.

"But first we need to talk about your stay here."

"My stay here." Ryan mumbles as he looks up from the floor at the doctor.

"As long as you are here, I will need you to remain calm. As long you can do that, we will have no reason to take any kind of precautions. Do you understand?"

My stay here, Ryan thinks, as he looks up at the doctor. "I understand, I will be okay." Ryan says.

At that moment, he is taken back in his mind to when his mother would take him to the local K-Mart and would give him the, you better behave or else speech before going in. Ryan comes out of his thought, "Yes, I understand." Ryan says again.

"Good...that's good." the doctor replies. "Now in a few minutes, we are going to move you to your room."

"My room?"

"Yes, your room." the doctor replies.

"How long do I have to stay here? And where is Amber?" Ryan asks calmly.

"We can talk about all that when you get to your room." the doctor replies. "Can you do that?"

Ryan nods his approval, knowing that if he reacts to what he is feeling inside, it is back in restraints for him. "Yes, I can do that." Ryan replies.

"Good." the doctor says, "That's good."

Within several minutes of their conversation, an orderly enters the room with a wheelchair. *A wheelchair…really! What the hell do I need a wheelchair for?* Ryan thinks, but says nothing, afraid of the doctor's and orderlies retaliation if he did. Ryan lifts himself off the table and sits in the wheelchair. As the orderly wheels him down the hallway to his "new home," he sees that some of the "patients" are sitting alone quietly, others pacing and removed from reality and some were behaving erratically. Ryan has no illusion of where he is now. *This is a crazy house and they think I'm crazy*, he thinks to himself.

As they roll him into his room, he sees that everything is white, and it is how he would picture it would be if he ever found himself in such a place. As he steps off the wheelchair, he sees the doctor is standing in the doorway but she does not come into the room.

"I am going to let you get settled in, and we can talk later," the doctor says.

Ryan does not reply, only nods as he moves around the thin sheet left for him on the concrete slab which substitutes for a bed, as she leaves the doorway. Ryan looks out the small window in the room. As he gazes out at the world, he thinks of what Amber is doing and where she is, how Buddy is doing and what he must be thinking of him not being there, but above all he thinks of how much he wishes he could see Sara again and hold her. He looks down at the floor. This is a quiet and sad moment that he will share with no one but himself.

CHAPTER
TWELVE

A new day has begun. Ryan awakens from his bed, the scratchy feel of the hospital sheets on his skin as he kicks out of them. As his bare feet touch the concrete floor a slight chill runs through his body. Ryan sighs. *Carpet would be nice he thinks.* Making his way to the bathroom he can hear the commotion outside his door as doctors, staff and patients all begin moving around, starting their day. Ryan washes his face and removes the morning from his eyes. Looking into the mirror, he is wondering why all of this has happened. Ryan dresses himself in what look like scrubs that have been left for him in the bathroom and walks out into the unknown. As he looks around, he is confused and not exactly sure what he is supposed to be doing. Ryan looks left then right and tries to formulate a plan, but he is hesitant to say or do anything that could constitute punishment so he stands there in silence. Finally he makes the decision to move, he follows to where he can hear the sound of a TV.

Ryan can see that the area where the TV is located is surrounded by people, mostly patients. Ryan quietly finds an empty chair and sits down. *I am not crazy, I don't belong here*, he thinks. He knows that even if his story sounds unbelievable, it does not make it any less true. All the people that surround him have legitimate psychological issues. *Not me*, he thinks. Suddenly he hears his name being called. Ryan turns to where the sound came from. He can see Dr. Fisher standing at the edge of the room. Ryan stares for a moment as she motions for him to come over to her. Ryan reluctantly gets out of the chair and slowly walks toward her.

"How are you doing?" she asks.

"Fine."

"Would you like to sit down and talk?"

"Yes, that's fine."

Although they are talking alone, he can see the orderlies standing in the distance, they are pretending like they are not there for him but in their eyes Ryan can see that secretly they are waiting for him to get out of line. The doctor begins to lead Ryan down the narrow hallway to her office; the orderlies following close behind, still trying to pretend they are not following them. Once inside the doctor's office, she tells Ryan, "Please, sit down."

Ryan complies but says nothing, taking a moment to look around the room.

"I know you have a lot of questions," the doctor says, "So let's start out by allowing you to ask one."

Ryan pauses, *Just one, I better make it good,* he thinks. He looks at the doctor and asks the most pressing question on his mind. "How long do I have to stay here?"

"That is totally up to you." she replies.

That is not an answer, Ryan thinks and stares at her intensely, *because if it were up to me I would be leaving right now.*

"We need to know that you are okay and in a good place both mentally and physically, before we make that determination. Do you understand?" the doctor asks as Ryan continues to stare.

"Yes." Ryan replies.

"Now let's talk about your dream, I believe you said the woman you were dreaming about was named…Sara, correct?"

"Yes," Ryan nods, his mind focusing on Sara's face and somehow drawing strength from her beauty. "Yes…Sara."

"What about Amber?" she asks.

Ryan looks down at the ground, a feeling of shame and embarrassment comes over him. "I love my wife,"

"But you love Sara too?"

Ryan hesitates. He wants to scream. He struggles to remain still in his chair. "Yes," he replies.

"Okay." the doctor replies, "Do you think Sara loves you?"

Ryan hesitates again, he knows what he wants to say but knows the consequences if he does. Ryan plays it safe, "I am not sure."

"Okay, do you think Amber loves you?" Ryan looks around the room. "Ryan, do you think Amber loves you?" The doctor repeats.

"Of course, she does! …How much longer do we have to do this?" Ryan asks as he fidgets in his chair and looks around wildly.

Dr. Fisher can see that Ryan is becoming agitated. She pauses for a moment, "That's enough for today. Let's pick this up here tomorrow."

Ryan exhales a sigh of relief. "Can I go now?"

"Yes, you can go."

The next several weeks, it is more of the same. Ryan's days have turned into an endless cycle of talks and therapy, but no matter how many sessions he has had and the progress they believe he is making, he knows they will not break him into believing that what he felt was not real, and no matter how hard they try, they would not be able to erase the feelings he has for Sara. Finally the day has come and Ryan is allowed a visitor, although he is torn and has mixed feelings about it, he is excited to see Amber.

As Ryan enters the visiting room, he can see that Amber is already there waiting. Ryan walks to the table where she is sitting. Amber turns and sees Ryan; she quickly gets to her feet and embraces him. Ryan looks at Amber and wipes the tears from her cheeks.

"How are you?" Amber asks.

"I'm fine." Ryan replies.

As they sit, Amber appears to have so many questions but seems content to just be at his side. As the two sit and make small talk, Amber looks at Ryan and asks, "The story you told me, do you believe it is real?"

Ryan pauses and looks down at the floor, knowing that if he says the wrong thing, things could go horribly wrong. "I'm not sure what I know," Ryan replies. "I am hoping they can fix me and send me home to you."

Amber smiles, "Of course they can… This is not your fault."

Ryan does not reply, he just sits quietly holding Amber's hand across the table. "No matter what happens, I love you." Ryan tells Amber. "I need you to know that."

Amber squeezes his hand. "I know that." she replies. "You need to do your best here and know that everything is going to be okay."

The visitors begin to slowly dwindle around them and Ryan knows their visit is coming to an end. As their final moments together come to close to an end, Amber's curiosity cannot contain itself and even though she knows it may go terribly wrong, she asks, "Are you still having dreams?"

Ryan quickly looks at Amber finding himself caught off guard, pausing and not sure how to respond, *I have hesitated too long,* he thinks. As he struggles for the answer and frantically searches for the right response in his mind, he looks away from Amber then around the room and says, "No, I have not had any more."

Amber's eyes are relieved but can't help but notice the change in Ryan. It is almost as if he is sad or disappointed that he has not had any more dreams. It is at the moment that she is certain that no matter how unbelievable his story was, he believes it to be true. Ryan stands as the orderlies are letting everyone know that visiting hours are over.

Amber gives Ryan one last embrace and a kiss. Ryan is thankful to have seen her, but in the midst of such conflict in his heart, it is almost sad that she came. Amber waves to Ryan as he leaves the room. She remains troubled by his reaction, so walks to Dr. Fisher's office and softly knocks on the door.

"Come in." says a voice says from inside.

Amber enters the room.

"Hello, Amber." Dr. Fisher says.

"Hello, Doctor. I don't mean to bother you but wanted to ask you how Ryan is doing?"

"Amber how are you?—Please, sit," the doctor tells Amber as she makes her way around to the front of the desk. The doctor pauses for a moment and looks at Amber with empathy. "Physically, Ryan is fine," the doctor tells Amber.

"And mentally?" Amber asks.

Dr. Fisher looks down at the floor then looks at Amber. "I'm not sure."

"What does that mean, you're not sure?"

"Ryan still believes the woman in his dreams is real," the doctor states as Amber pauses.

"But she is real." Amber replies.

The doctor, with a look of bewilderment on her face, says, "I beg your pardon?"

"I mean she is a real person. She is a patient in the hospital, she is on the same floor where Ryan was while he was in a coma."

The doctor still with a look of confusion, "This hospital?" she asks.

"Yes." Amber replies, "And I think she is the key to all this."

"How is that?" the doctor asks.

"I don't know, but I think I need to find out for all us. It is either Ryan and this woman were having an affair, or what Ryan is saying is true, no matter how unbelievable it sounds."

"You know that is not possible, right?" the doctor states.

"Truthfully doctor, I don't know what to believe." Amber says, "But I do know that I have to do everything I can to help Ryan even if it …even if it destroys us." Amber states.

The doctor looks intently at Amber, "Before you do this there is just one thing you need to do," the doctor says.

Amber looks at the doctor, "What?" she asks.

"Please make sure that you really want to know." Amber tilts her head back looking up at the ceiling and pauses, but before Amber can reply the doctor says, "because once you know you can't erase it, and good or bad it will then belong to you." Amber says nothing and begins to walk out of the room; Amber briefly looks back at the doctor as they share a last glance through the partially open door before it closes.

CHAPTER

THIRTEEN

A mber stands in the hallway looking back through the partially open door where Dr. Fisher is, still standing in front of her desk obviously perplexed by what was said. It is the most foreboding feeling Amber has ever felt in her life. The sounds of the people moving around her are cluttered by her thoughts but are the sounds she can clearly identify. Amber stands in silence as everyone is moving around her. It is as if she is a fixed boulder in a stream of flowing water and everyone and everything is flowing around her. She wants to move, scream, cry, anything but is paralyzed by her thoughts. *Which one is it?* Amber thinks, *is my husband somehow involved with this woman in a seedy affair to which she is angered to the point of madness, or I have lost him to some sort of mental illness with no way to help him. Because the dream thing cannot be real!*

She stands there, unsure of what she has to do. *Where do I begin?* Amber ponders. She comes back to the moment, knowing she must be strong, but for now must find the strength to leave the hospital. As she walks across the parking lot, she looks back at the hospital rooms. In one of them, the woman at the center of all this. Although she feels sympathy for the woman and her condition, she is angered by what may have taken place and how that has changed the course of her life and marriage. *What if what she suspects is true?* she thinks. Amber looks away and gets into the truck and begins to drive home, her thoughts heavy; the tightness in her neck is almost to the point of pain.

As she drives along, she sees a sparkle through the corner of her eye. Her eyes track to the source of the shimmer. In the partially open ashtray, she sees a small section of chain dangling from it. She has been using Ryan's truck since he was committed and has no idea what it might be or never noticed it before. Her curiosity peaked she reaches for the small section of chain, touching it as it swings from left to right. Amber opens the ashtray and pulls out the small piece of the chain. *It is a necklace,* she thinks as she pulls it from its resting place. Amber holds up the necklace and sees that it has a heart-shaped pendant with a jewel at its center. Amber ponders where it could have come from? She knew that she did not own such a piece of jewelry and could not imagine what Ryan would be doing with it. *There has to be a simple explanation,* she thinks, then her thoughts turn to the only logical conclusion, Sara.

As she feels tears collecting in her eyes and without thought she places the necklace in her purse and continues home, all the while consumed with denial, *this cannot be,* she thinks. As she pulls into the driveway, she hurriedly opens the truck door and makes her way to the house, ignoring Buddy who is waiting on the porch. She tosses her purse and keys onto the kitchen table and makes her way to the computer. As she logs on, her mind is filled with an endless possibility and scenarios she herself can't even accept. The computer comes to life as she moves the cursor arrow around in a frantic pattern, her thoughts not allowing her to concentrate. Amber takes a breath and allows her hand to guide the arrow to the history tab. She clicks and looks at recent history, she wants to know the last thing Ryan was looking at, and the article with Sara's story appears.

As she begins to read the article, she learns that the accident occurred not too far from the house. Her mind begins to build a case for affair as these small bits of information are taking shape into an obvious case to convict. *What was she doing so close to the house? And how could she know where we live?* Amber thinks, putting aside any other alternate explanation. She continues to read as the article lays out who Sara was and what happened the night of the accident. A portion of the article tells that Sara was on her way home that evening and was to have been celebrating her ten-year wedding anniversary the following day. Amber is taken back when the article details that Sara and her husband were to have been on a romantic trip to Costa Rica for their anniversary. Also in the article a specific place in Costa Rica was mentioned, a place familiar to Amber—the Manuel Antonio Beach. Amber pauses and thinks of their trip to Costa Rica and how distant Ryan was the entire time they were there almost as if he was wishing he was there with someone else. Could Ryan have told Sara about this trip and the reason she was spending her anniversary there? *This can't be a coincidence*, she thinks as the mountain of possible evidence grows in her mind.

Amber sits back in the chair, unwilling to go on any further. Her heart is breaking in two, and the betrayal now resting upon her is insurmountable. Amber can feel herself becoming nauseous and is finding it difficult to breath. She pushes away from the desk and makes her way to the bathroom, forcing open the door. She rummages through the medicine cabinet, looking frantically for anything to ease her state of mind. Amber sees a bottle of the painkillers given to Ryan after his accident on the shelf. She reaches for the bottle, grabbing it knocking everything else off the shelf onto the counter and into the sink. She struggles to open the bottle, her anger and panic is causing her hands to shake. She manages to get the bottle open, shaking one pill onto her open hand. She looks at the pill and continues to shake the bottle as second pill falls out, then a third, then all of them. *End it all?* She thinks. She looks into the mirror, the face looking back is sad, but not to the point of self-ending despair. She hesitates, finally pouring all but two of the pills back into the bottle and closes it. Amber places the few remaining pills into her mouth, turns on the water, and using her hand she scoops, the water into her mouth, tilting her head back and swallows. Amber places both hands on the sink counter and stares into the mirror.

Telling herself and asking "You are so stupid! How could you be so stupid?" In her anger she strikes the mirror, shattering it. Amber's mind is beyond her control now; her anger has built to a boil. Amber leaves the bathroom and makes her way to the bedroom. She looks around the room, not sure of what she is looking for. In her rage she begins to open the drawers to Ryan's nightstand reaching in and throwing everything onto the floor. She does the same thing to the dresser then the closet. She wants to find more, she is sure there is more. Finally she tires, falling onto the bed crying uncontrollably and screaming, "How could you do this to me, Ryan? Why would you do this?"

Amber lays there motionless and eventually falls asleep, exhausted by her thoughts and actions. She is awakened by the sunlight of a new day, and although she slept, she is exhausted. She struggles to get out of bed, still dressed in the clothing that she had on the night before. Amber finally makes her way to the living room and sits on the couch, unsure what she is going to do now. Lost, she desperately tries to make sense of it all as she covers her face with her hands. Buddy comes to the couch, he knows that something is wrong and sits by her side quietly, the look of wanting to help in his eyes but with no way to transfer that into action. Amber sits for a while and suddenly thinks, *Charlie.*

Amber reaches for the phone and dials. The phone rings and Charlie answers.

"Hello."

"Hey, Charlie, it's me, Amber."

"Amber?" Charlie replies. "How are you?" he asks.

"I'm good." Amber replies, but before Charlie has an opportunity to say more, she says to Charlie, "Listen I need to ask you something." Amber says.

"Sure, what is it?"

Without warning or a dramatic buildup, Amber pointedly asks, "Charlie, was Ryan having an affair?"

"What...An affair? ...What are you talking about?"

"Yes, Charlie, an affair...was Ryan having an affair?"

"Look I have no idea what you are talking about, but Ryan would never cheat on you." Charlie emphatically replies. "That's crazy—Why would you think that?"

"Tell me the truth, Charlie!" Amber shouts. "I need to hear the truth."

"Amber, I have no idea what is going on, but Ryan wouldn't do that." Charlie states.

Amber pulls the phone down, looks at the keypad, and begins to hang up. She can hear Charlie saying "Amber...Amber, are you there?" as the phone goes silent. Amber sits for a moment, still consumed with wanting to know the truth and finding anything to prove its existence. Amber pulls herself together and cleans herself up. She grabs her keys and purse and heads out the front door, not even bothering to lock it. She gets into the truck and starts to drive to the hospital. Amber is sure of what she is doing and is confident in what she has learned, driven by her determination to get to the bottom of it all is resolute as she continues to drive.

Amber pulls into the parking lot, however, she now finds herself having doubts. *This can't be true. Ryan would not have done this. I know it*, she thinks, but her logic tells her that she is completely correct in her assumptions. Amber gets out of the truck and begins to walk into the hospital. She is unsure of what she will say, but she has to see this woman for herself. As she enters the hospital, the nursing staff sees her and greets her.

"Coming to see Ryan?" they ask.

Amber smiles but offers no reply. Amber stares down the hallway to where Ryan is and turns to the elevator. Her mind focuses on the numbers of the floor indicator. She watches as it counts down, 3…2…1. She stands there as the doors open, still staring up at the indicator. She is jolted back to reality as a male voice asks, "Ma'am, are you getting on?" Amber apologizes and gets on the elevator.

"What floor?" the same voice asks. Amber stands there in silence distracted by her thought and says nothing. The voice asks again, "Ma'am, what floor?"

She interrupts his question and replies, "Five."

She watches as the floor indicator lights up, 2…3…4… Amber's heart is pounding as the elevator moves closer to the floor she selected; she can feel the walls of the elevator closing in, causing her to become claustrophobic. The doors open as the indicator reads 5. Amber pushes past the people in the elevator and stands in the hallway relieved that she has more air to breathe. She hesitantly makes her way down the hallway; it is eerily quiet. Her heart is in her throat, and she is experiencing a level of discomfort she never knew existed. As she approaches the room, she can see the bed and the blond hair of the woman laying on it. She can also see a man sitting on a chair next to the bed. Amber finds herself standing at the doorway.

The man, somehow sensing that she is there, turns to Amber and asks, "Can I help you?"

It is too late now, Amber thinks. "My name is Amber." She softly says.

The man rises out of the chair, a puzzled look on his face. "Do I know you?"

"No…not really. I mean my husband was on this same floor with your wife."

"Who is your husband?"

"Ryan…His name is Ryan,"

"Ryan." Albert says looking up at the ceiling as he searches his memory then repeats, "Ryan, oh yes Ryan. He was here one time and introduced himself to me." Amber just stares.

"My name is Albert."

"It is nice to meet you Albert."

They both stand in silence for a moment, Amber's eyes begin filling up with tears that do not go unnoticed.

"Are you okay?" Albert asks.

Amber pauses not sure of what or how to say what she has come there to say. "I came here to ask you something."

"Okay, sure, what is it?"

Amber struggles to find the right words until finally she blurts out, "Do you know if your wife and my husband were having an affair?"

Albert laughs, "What?" he asks in confusion and disbelief. "Why would you ask me something like that?" Albert responds, the sound of anger in his voice.

Amber thinks about what she is about to say, knowing that if she says it, she will be fully committed to whatever happens next.

Amber takes a deep breath; "My husband told me about a dream he had about your wife and that in this dream he was having an affair with your wife."

Albert stands not sure of what he just heard even though he is certain of it, "That is absurd!" Albert responds.

"I know this sounds crazy." Amber tries to say.

Albert quickly interrupts her, "You are asking me this because of a dream your husband had? My wife is in a coma and has been in a coma for a long time. I would know if she was having an affair which she was most certainly not, how could she? I think you need to leave."

"I'm sorry." Amber says, "I don't want to be here, and I don't want to be asking you these questions."

"Then why are you?"

"My husband has been committed to the psychiatric ward of this hospital because of this dream."

"Well there you go, your husband's crazy, now get the hell out of here."

"I can't!" Amber replies, "I have to find out what is going on."

"Nothing, that's what's going on."

"Look! My husband was becoming mentally unstable to the point he is now committed to this hospital and I think the reason is this dream. I think my husband's accident caused him to think it was a dream when in reality he was having an affair or it is a dream and your wife somehow is part of it. Either way, there has to be some connection between your wife and my husband."

"That is the craziest thing I have ever heard." Albert responds.

"As crazy as this sounds, I think my husband believes he loves your wife." Amber says in I raised tone. "I know how all this sounds but if my husband was having an affair then he can be helped but if not then he..." she pauses. "Your wife's accident was close to our home, right?" Amber asks.

"What does that have to do with anything?"

"Why was she there?"

"She was on her way home."

"Why would Ryan come to see your wife if he did not know her?" Amber asks drawing at straws with all of her questions. Albert looks at Amber with curiosity thinking there are a lot of coincidences. With a long pause Amber finally says, "Ryan knew your wife's name, how do you explain all this unless they knew each other?"

Albert pauses not sure what to think of all he has just heard and with no other response says, "You're basing all this on a dream and where the accident happened? And on top of all that, your husband knew my wife's name? This is crazy!"

"Please, I am not trying to upset you or trouble you. I just need to know if you think or ever suspected that they knew one another."

"Look lady, I don't know why you are doing this, but you need to get the hell out of here right now!" Albert says in a menacing tone.

Amber stares at Albert unmoved by the crazed look in his eyes. Amber turns and moves toward the door, and as she approaches it, she looks back at Sara then glances to the floor before looking back at Albert. Amber turns and faces Albert, takes a deep breath and asks, "Have you ever seen this before?" she asks, her hand now inside her purse moving about searching the darkness of its recesses.

Albert stands fixated on her hand's movement, curiously wondering what she was doing, not knowing what, if anything, she was going to show him. Ambers hand slowly emerges as the necklace that Amber found in Ryan's truck comes into the light. Albert moves slowly forward, a look of disbelief on his face, the pendant of the necklace moving from left to right.

"Where did you get that?" he asks with tears building up in his voice.

"It was in my husband's truck."

"That's impossible." Albert says under his breath, he moves closer for a better look but knows what he is looking at. "It belongs to Sara. We could not find it the day of her accident. She wore it everywhere, she never took it off." Albert reaches out slowly and touches the necklace his eyes wide with confusion he whispers, "It was her mother's."

Amber with pause says, "If you are telling me that my husband and your wife never knew each other and they could have never possibly been having an affair, then how could he have this? Why would my husband destroy his life and throw away ours if all of this wasn't true? If that is what you are saying, then I guess all of us are dreaming then, aren't we?" Amber says.

CHAPTER
FOURTEEN

lbert is left in silence, his thoughts racing out of control with nothing and no one there to help him slow them down. The world he thought he knew has now unmistakably forced him upon a precipice, to which he teeters on the thought that no matter how unbelievable, it might be true. Albert stands in the ominous glow of the lowly lit room; he stares at Sara and begins to feel himself fill up with tears, something he was not even aware he could do.

Albert by all accounts was considered to be a "good man." and was a friendly and outgoing guy; however, at home, the story was quite different. Albert and Sara had been married for ten years and within those years there were many mixed periods of good times and long durations of bad ones. Albert, a self-proclaimed workaholic, loved what he did and for the last eight years made his money by selling medical supplies; however his fun and charismatic personality which made him successful was limited to work and did not carry into his marriage to Sara, which developed into a long history, and even a habit, of taking Sara for granted. It was a confirmed fact that at times Albert was verbally abusive to Sara but never to the point of physical violence; however even with that being the case, one can argue that emotional pain in some cases is more painful than any physical punishment one can endure. Because of Albert's work schedule and the sheer nature of his profession, there were many long days and nights that prevented Albert from spending more time with Sara. Not to mention Albert's extracurricular activities that carried him into a world of infidelity and drinking. It could be said that Sara knew what her husband was like and was aware of the countless women who had entered and exited his life, but she held onto the hope that love in some way or the other would conquer all.

In a strange way, Sara's wish was granted on the day of her accident. But even though Albert's escapades were dramatically slowed after the accident, in reality he had not changed, but for the sake of the onlookers he now played the role of a concerned and devoted husband. Which makes you wonder why or maybe explains why he was so offended and angered when Amber revealed what she thought she knew about his wife, and how she could have been having an affair with her husband. It could be argued that Albert's thought at that moment was, *What is good for the goose is not always good for the gander.* As Albert collects his thoughts he is consumed by the possibilities in front of him and even though he himself thought it to be a hypocritical thought thinks, H*ow could Sara do this, that bitch,* he thinks. *How could she do this to me? She is nothing without me.*

Albert unwillingly begins to follow along in Amber's journey of trying to figure out what was true or not true, and he finds himself wondering down the hallway, thinking, *What do* I do?—*What could I do?* Albert slowly walks and thinks of what Amber said and without thought wanders to the mental illness ward of the hospital. In his mind Albert is angered but he is not necessarily sure if it is for the reason you would think. As he approaches the ward he sees that not just anyone can enter. An identification badge or code would be necessary to enter to which he had neither; a precaution of course, and quite possibly for a moment just like this one. Albert stands at the doorway, peering through the small rectangular windows of the door.

By chance Ryan happens to be in the direct line of sight of Albert; however, Ryan does not see him. Albert stares with intensity at Ryan, trying to image the man that he is staring at could be the same man involved with his wife. Finally Ryan turns in the direction of the doorway where Albert is standing. It does not right away register in Ryan's mind that he is even looking at him, the small window offering only a sliver as to the identity of the person just beyond it. Ryan somehow senses he is being watched and begins to focus on the person who is obviously looking directly at him, Ryan pauses, and in that moment he realizes that it is Albert. Ryan's thoughts race as he ponders why he would be standing there. *Was Sara okay? What does he want?* As the stares from Albert begin to spark understanding in Ryan's mind, he can somehow feel why he is there. *He knows,* Ryan thinks, as he sees Albert finally break his stare, look down at the floor and walks out of view.

Albert walks back down the hallway, his curiosity now at a boil. *I have to know!* He frantically thinks, *Should I go back to the room, and confront Sara? Ridiculous of course, she is in a coma he thinks to himself, The house?... What about the house?* If I am looking for answers, they must be there, so he abandons his journey back to his wife's side and gets on the elevator.

Albert makes his way to his home; and begins to manically search through the house, looking for any trace of the affair that Sara is accused of but finds nothing. Every open drawer, every upturned piece of furniture, another fruitless search. In a sort of desperate attempt Albert picks up the phone as if to call someone. He stands there for a moment with the receiver in his hand, he has no one to call, who could he call, and even if he had someone to call what would he say? Albert puts the phone down and leaves his home, his eyes glazed over with no idea what to do, his hands wringing over the steering wheel as he drives. Suddenly with no other possibilities he thinks, *Amber! Why not, she would know more than anyone, but where does Amber live?* then Albert remembers that Amber told him they lived close to the place where Sara had her accident and also remembers Ryan saying the same when they met.

Albert drives in the direction of the accident site and as he is coming up to the spot where the accident happened he sees another vehicle parked alongside the road. Albert approaches slowly, trying to make out the figure standing outside the truck. It is a woman, and as the figure takes shape, he realizes that the shape is a familiar one, it is Amber. Albert stops the car and gets out. Amber immediately recognizes it is Albert but does not react. He walks over to where she is standing, the two remain silent for a moment.

Finally Amber speaks, "You know that it has to be true right?"

Albert says nothing, staring down at the ground, his eyes focus on the discolored ground where the fire occurred.

Amber takes a deep breath as she stares out across the adjacent field, "I have combed through the phone, the computer, the house, the trash... If they were having an affair they were careful."

Albert responds and explains how he, too, has torn apart their lives looking for any hint of the affair, but there was nothing to be found.

"How do you think that is possible?" Amber asks.

Both Albert and Amber stand there in silence. Both at a complete loss what to do next. Albert breaks the uncomfortable silence and asks, "Would you like to get a cup of coffee?"

Amber looks at him with a sort of thankfulness, his kind gesture a welcomed but strange comfort, after all their spouses were potentially having an affair, it gets no stranger than that you would think. Amber turns to Albert, a small smile and laugh.

"We can go in my car." Albert says.

She offers no reply but begins to move toward his car finally standing by the passenger door. Albert opens the door for Amber and closes it. Albert looks over the roof of the car, unsure what to think of what is happening. As they drive along, they begin to talk about their lives. Amber tells the tale of her and Ryan, to which Albert follows suit with the tales of his romance with Sara, finally arriving at their destination. Over the next several hours they sit in a small coffee shop in town talking about a variety of topics. Then without warning the rain begins to fall, Amber looks out the window and sighs. *I am happy it is raining, now we can stay longer*, she thinks, as they continue to talk. As the rain shimmers down the window they continue their search, each one picking apart their lives and looking for any traces of what they may have missed. As the time passes, they find themselves having a deeper and, in some respect, more intimate conversation. It could be said that it was the stress of all that had happened, or a need for some tiny bit of human contact between two lost souls that brought about the change. No matter what the reason, it is becoming apparent that the eye contact and body language they are giving to one another are more than heartbreak and tragedy, but instead taking the shape of attraction. She finds herself looking at Albert in a way she knows she shouldn't. His strong build, green eyes and jet black hair generating feelings she had only felt with Ryan. This is all confirmed when at one point during their strange encounter, Albert reaches across the table covering Amber's hand with his own.

Amber's first thought is to pull away, but it has been so long since someone has touched her in that way, so she does not move. But after a few moments, she stares at Albert and gently pulls her hand from beneath Albert's.

"I have to go." Amber says.

"Where?" Albert replies, gazing into Amber's eyes.

"I can't do this." she remarks as she get up from the table.

Albert quickly stands up. "Wait."

"For what?" Amber replies, "How can we even think of what is happening between us now, that is, how we ended up here to begin with!" Amber says in a raised tone. "Our families have been destroyed because of what might have happened between them, so how can we?" Amber says as she fills with emotion.

Albert says nothing and follows Amber as she walks out of the coffee shop. Albert reaches for Amber's arm as she walks away. She pauses but does not turn around, her heart is breaking and now compounded by the guilt that she feels for the way she is feeling for Albert. As they step out into the street, the rain streaming down both their faces.

"Why are we the guilty ones?—They had an affair on us,"

Amber turns, the rain streaming down her face, her tears concealed by the rain and says, "Who would we be if we did the same?"…
"Would two wrongs somehow make it right?"

"That is a not good enough answer Amber!" Albert shouts.

"Of course it is, it has to be enough," Amber replies as she stares at Albert. "So they just get away with it, is that how it works? So what we want doesn't matter?" Amber says nothing more and without further debate gets into the car. Albert stares at Amber through the rain covered windshield then gets into the car.

As they drive back to Amber's truck, Amber stares out the window. She is not sure what, or if there is anything to say and in some ways does not want to add to what has already happened.

"Are you okay?" Albert asks.

Amber nods. "I'm just tired."

Albert continues to drive. The sound of the windshield wipers clearing the way is the only sound that can be heard. As they arrive back at the truck Albert asks, "Can I call you?" Amber looks at him with skepticism and pauses, Albert backpedals and says, "If I find anything?"

Amber just looks away as she exits the car. Albert gets out as She closes the door and begins to walk to the truck. He says nothing and just watches as Amber opens the truck door. She pauses then turns to him, "If you find anything, you can just come by the house. I am the fourth house on the right when you turn on Saw Mill Road."

Albert says nothing as he watches Amber get into the truck and drive past him.

A few weeks go by with no interaction between Albert and Amber, each one too busy being consumed with tearing their lives apart and piecing them back together with the hopes of finding the truth. Although they have not seen or talked to each other in weeks they both find themselves thinking of one another and how their chance meeting could have been something more. Then one day, Buddy is unexplainably barking. Amber, standing in the kitchen, dismisses his alert, then she hears a familiar voice through the screen door. Amber pauses and thinks, *Albert*. As she turns, the silhouette of Albert comes into view, He's peering through the screen door.

"Hi." Albert says.

"Hello," Amber replies as she moves toward the door.

"How are you?" He asks.

"I've been okay."

"May I come in?"

Amber hesitates, unsure of what to do. She slowly opens the door, nods her head and says, "Yes, of course, come in."

As Albert steps into the living room, Amber distances herself, cautious of the stranger in her home.

"I just wanted to stop by and see how you were doing."

"I have been better." Amber replies. "So you have found something?"

"No, nothing." Albert replies. "Have you found anything?"

"I have looked through every piece of paper in this house, I have looked in every drawer, under every bed, and in every possible hiding spot I could think of and have found nothing." Amber replies. "The only proof I have is my husband's story and your wife's necklace."

Albert stares down at the floor, "It can't be true, right? …Your husband's story?"

"I am not sure what I believe anymore." Amber replies as she too, looks at the floor, the strange feeling of attraction between them is like a giant elephant in the room.

The two stand as statues, unsure of the next move. Finally Amber says, "I have a lot to do today."

"Oh, okay." Albert replies as he senses that means goodbye. Albert turns to the door and replies, "Me too. I need to get some things done before I get back to the hospital."

Amber continues to stare at the floor as Albert grabs hold of the handle of the screen door. "It was nice seeing you again," Amber says, unconsciously moving toward the door.

"It was nice seeing you." Albert replies. Now just a few inches apart Albert asks, "What do we do now?"

"I don't know."

Albert carefully reaches out his hand and takes Amber's hand. She does not pull away and rubs her finger on his hand. The two look up at each other and without thought lean toward each other, their lips gently touching as Buddy looks on, unsure what to make of what is happening.

Amber pulls away, "You better go."

"Okay."

Amber watches as Albert steps off the porch and walks to his car. For reasons she cannot explain, she wants to stop him. She knows that he, too, wants to stay. *But how can we? How can I?* she thinks. Albert opens the door to the car and stands in silence, staring at Amber who has walked out onto the porch. He stands there waiting, like a tiger awaiting some small opportunity to pounce. Amber stands there staring at Albert, and he back at her. Finally the silence is broken as Amber hesitantly says,

"Anytime you would like to come by, you can."

He smiles, "I'll do that, so that means see you later, right?"

Amber nods yes as Albert opens the car door still looking at Amber. He gets in and closes the car door. Amber knows what she has done. She knows that if Albert returns, it will be more than a gentle kiss on the lips. She is certain that if he comes back, he will be more than she can resist. As she watches Albert's car drive out of sight she thinks, *Why do I feel guilty? Ryan was the one having an affair even if I am unable to find the smoking gun. Why should I not be able to find love with someone else if Ryan did?* As she continues to debate with herself. Then Amber's thoughts turn to Ryan and Sara who have both suffered and are continuing to suffer from the tragic events which have left them damaged and broken.

As Amber goes back into the house, she feels a horrible sense of loneliness and fear. She is now in the midst of the most impossible of situations, a possible love affair between her husband and the woman whose husband she now feels is headed in the same direction. Even though she is justifying everything in her mind that this is okay.

But no matter the justification Amber knows that if this happens it would not be a dream, because if discovered it would only be the start of a nightmare.

CHAPTER
FIFTEEN

I t has been an unusual chain of events that has led each of them to this odd moment in time, a place filled with tragedy, luck, betrayal, and love. Each one of them finds themselves one of many moving parts of what has become a monstrous machine grinding them into submission. As Amber sits at her kitchen table, she stares out into the open field across the road from her home, her mind filled with the many things she has done, should do, and might do. Amber feels her hands firmly grasp the coffee cup on both sides and she slowly and gently sips the coffee, the steam bellows out like an old-time steam engine. She smiles and takes comfort in the fact that with all that has happened at the very least, she met Albert and for a brief moment, felt something she thought she could never feel for anyone but Ryan.

Albert steps out of the hospital room where he is at Sara's side. He leans with his back against the wall just outside the doorway and he finds himself staring up at the ceiling. His thoughts are divided, his first to the woman lying just twenty feet from him, helpless and unaware. Then to the man down the hallway who has or may have been a part of her life in ways he cannot accept. Then finally to Amber, the woman who came into his life and touched his heart, may it be by circumstance or sheer luck. She has made him feel things he never thought he could. Sadly, he also knows that she is responsible for bringing along with her the potentially tragic news that has changed their lives. Albert looks down at the floor a strange feeling of love, comes over him. *How could all this be possible,* he thinks, *Why?*

Ryan sits quietly in his room and finds himself gripped with fear in his mind. The crippling thoughts and emotions punishing him with a relentless assault. Ryan thinks of Amber who has stood by him through all of this, then to Albert, whose strange visit outside the hospital ward doors has left him with a sense of not knowing why he was there but having some idea. Finally Sara and his longing to see her. Together all of these are facets that leave him faced with an unbearable and insurmountable summit he is forced to climb. He feels himself losing touch with reality his mind taking him to places he is not sure he wants to follow. His thoughts so clear it is as if a person was standing in front of him speaking to him. Ryan looks at his reflection in the window and sees a ghostly shell of a man that once was.

He has not showered in days, the bags under his eyes and unshaven appearance are evidence of his lack of caring or opinion of the world around him. Ryan turns away from what he is looking at and finds himself faced with the grim reality that the numerous counseling sessions, medications, and other treatments are not working. They have all failed to erase the love he feels for what they say is a figment of his imagination. Ryan finds himself in a strange search, a search not of a way to repair the damage between him and Amber or even how to deal with his current situation. Instead a search of how can he get back to Sara and what he must do to see her again. He continues to ponder the possibilities; however, every possibility, no better than the last. Ryan thinks to a conversation he had with a patient several weeks earlier who told him jokingly, "If you want to get out of here you are going to have to kill yourself." *What if I tried?* Ryan thinks, Or *what if I close enough to put myself into a coma like Sara?... How could you think such a thing?* he says to himself, *What if you fail?*

Amber gathers herself together, *I need to hurry and get out of the house, Ryan is probably waiting and wondering where I am,* she thinks. Amber prepares herself for the day, she is not entirely sure, but she has a feeling visitation day will not be a happy one. Stepping out of the shower she looks into the bathroom mirror and wipes away the steam. She is tired, her face showing the signs of the battle she has fought and that continues to rage on. Amber places her hands of the edge of the sink to help steady herself and to help stop them from trembling. She leaves the house, on her way to see Ryan, *Will I see Albert there?* she thinks, a strange thought in and of itself. The but-terfly sensation in her stomach is apparent as she's thinking that she will. Her sensation immediately alerts her to the feelings of guilt she knows are there but is ignoring. Amber is terrified of the feelings she is experiencing and what she will or would not do with them.

As she drives along, she realizes that no matter what happens, it almost feels like fate, so she continues on. As she pulls into the hospital parking lot she hesitates and wonders if she should go in at all. Amber is daunted by the thought that the building in front of her houses more emotions than one person should be subjected to in a lifetime. Amber sighs and exits the truck. The walk to the front door is a long one and as she makes her way to Ryan, a strange feeling of dread comes over her, it is almost one of not wanting to see Ryan. As she is allowed into the ward, Ryan sees Amber first and starts making his way toward her. Amber does not know it, but Ryan is sharing the same feeling of not wanting to see her. They both stand staring at one another, but just for a moment, then a small peck on the cheek and a courteous hug is all that remains to do before their visit begins. As they sit together, even small talk appears to be difficult today.

Finally, Ryan says, "Do you know who was outside the ward the other day?"

"Who?"

"That guy, Albert."

"Albert?" Amber replies, looking at the ground. "Albert who? The man with the wife in a coma, whose wife you are dreaming about?" Amber remarks, in a desperate attempt on her part to hide her own misdeeds.

"Yes, don't start!" Ryan says. "I wonder what he wanted."

"Who knows?" Amber replies, never making eye contact with Ryan.

"What's wrong?" Ryan asks.

"Nothing is wrong." Amber replies. "Why are you asking?" Amber says defensively.

Ryan in unsure why but he can sense that Amber seemed to be uneasy and almost uncomfortable when he mentioned Albert. Amber now appears to be nervous or frightened and after so many years of marriage he knows she is hiding something; somewhere in his mind, it is telling him to press on with finding out what it is. Ryan, out of nowhere, asks Amber, "Have you met him?" Ryan pauses and thinks, "Wait a minute, how did you know that is who I was talking about?" "What?" Amber replies. "A minute ago, you said the man whose wife is in a coma. How did you know it was him?"

Amber plays it off, a clueless look on her face, "Who, the man?"

"Yes, the man, Albert." he says as he leans closer to Amber, now in interrogation mode.

Amber knows that she should say the opposite of what is about to come out of her mouth, but she seems to not have the ability. "Yes, I met him."

Ryan sits back into his chair, unsure of why he feels this is a problem. "When?"

"Several weeks ago." Amber replies, her answer to the point offering little detail.

"And?"

"And what?... I talked to him."

"About what?" Ryan says. "Did you talk to him about me?"

"Sort of." Amber replies looking down at the floor.

"Okay, what does 'sort of' mean,—what did you tell him, Amber?"

Amber pauses, "About what you told me?"

"Why would you do that, Amber!" Ryan says in a raised tone. "You had no right to do that." Ryan says as he stands up, towering over Amber.

Amber's blood surges. She will not take this sitting down and swiftly gets out of her chair, now face-to-face with Ryan. "I had every right to do that. You tell me you're in love with a woman in your dreams and what? I'm just supposed to sit around and pretend like everything is okay?"

Ryan stands there with no sense of what to do, or say. "You are not to talk to him anymore." Ryan declares.

Amber is furious, the tears in her eyes clouding her vision. "You can't tell me who I can or can't talk to, Ryan!"

"I can and I just did."

"What are you afraid of?" Amber shouts. "Afraid that he has listened to me more than you?"

Ryan takes a step back. "Listened to you? You have talked to him more than once?"

Amber knows that she has said too much, so she looks away and chooses not to reply.

Ryan filled with rage, says, "Is that why he was here? So, was he looking for me or you?"

Amber looks up at Ryan not sure what to say. Ryan looks at Amber, looks away, and looks at her again. It is in that moment he realizes that he knows the look on Amber's face…it is the same look he sees in himself when he's thinking of Sara. "You need to leave."

"Ryan, please." Amber whispers.

"Leave!" Ryan shouts as he shoves the chair toward her.

Amber says nothing and slowly leaves the ward, her heart is broken in so many ways, she cannot even imagine. Amber spills out into the hallway, she feels disoriented and nauseous and as she stands in the hallway, she thinks, *What did I do?* As she begins to walk away from the ward, she sees Albert is at the end of the hallway standing there as if he was ready to rescue her. Albert sees Amber and makes his way toward her. Albert reaches for her as she melts into his arms.

"Are you okay?" Albert asks.

"No." Amber replies. "No, I am not okay."

"Come on, I'll take you home."

Albert walks Amber out of the hospital and helps Amber into his car and they drive away.

"What happened?" Albert asks.

"I don't want to talk about it." Amber replies. Albert turns his eye back to the road and leaves it alone.

As they arrive at Amber's house, Albert helps Amber into the front door. She feels weak in his arms. As they enter the door, Amber turns, thrusting her lips against Albert's. He does not reject her advances, and they begin a passionate kiss, and frantically begin tugging at each other's clothing. The momentum of their embrace pushes them into the kitchen as they continue to embrace and kiss. All at once their passion forces them against the kitchen counter. Amber breaths heavily and is desperately trying to unfasten Albert's belt and pants. As she opens them to what she thinks is enough, Amber reaches into them and feels that Albert is throbbing with excitement. Albert turns Amber around facing away from him, Amber's hands firmly on the counter as she stabilizes herself against it. Albert kisses the back of Amber's neck while he tries to pull down Amber's pants and panties; as he struggles they become tangled together adding to the erotic moment to which he now finds himself. Albert forces

Amber over the counter rubbing his hands against her back. Amber is now breathing even heavier, her hair covering her face as she turns from left to right as it rests against the counter. Albert rubs his hand down Amber's back and onto her buttocks. Amber arches her back, "Albert." she softly whispers….as Albert penetrates her. Their bodies in unison, as Albert begins to thrust over and over again. Amber screams in passion begging Albert not to stop, her hands sliding back and forward on the counter. Albert hesitates, he can feel his climax getting closer but does not want to stop. Suddenly Amber gasps as she feels Albert's discharge deep inside of her. They both slump forward onto the counter their heavy breathing the only sound other than the whimpering of Buddy who has no idea what is happening.

*****

Ryan sits in his room, consumed by everything. His mind fights against what he is thinking, but his only other thought is getting back to Sara. *My wife is doing God knows what. I am stuck in this place, they will never let me leave*, Ryan thinks, his mind is racing faster than he can keep pace. His depression and mania have blended together taking him to a place in his mind he has never been before. He is now in the recesses of his mind in which the opening is getting smaller and smaller. As he sits on the edge of the bed, without thought, he finds himself tearing at the bedsheet, the long slivers of fabric folding onto the floor.

Ryan stares straight ahead, his eyes fixed on a small spot on the wall across from him; it is almost if he is avoiding looking at what he is creating. The minutes go by so slowly he can hear the hands of the clock ticking like loud drumbeats as the seconds and minutes go by. The tearing of the sheet is complete, Ryan ties a slipknot in the fabric, he thinks back to when his father taught him to use such a knot when securing things on the bed of the truck. Ryan sits for a moment in silence his hands wringing over the strips of cloth. His eyes begin to fill up with tears as he places the noose over his head and tightens its grip around his neck. Ryan looks toward the door nervous that someone may unexpectedly come up to the window or come in. He methodically ties the other end of the sheet to the bed rail, giving him just enough slack to slide off the bed. *There is no turning back now,* he thinks, but is sure this is what he wants to do.

As Ryan slides off the bed, he can feel the weight of his body pulling on the noose and as he makes it to the floor, he sits there thinking, *This doesn't even hurt.* Ryan feels himself beginning to struggle, his body naturally trying to get air in as the noose cuts off its path. Ryan struggles to stay seated on the floor, and can feel himself losing consciousness as his body violently shakes he can feel the foam accumulating in the corner of his mouth. As he continues to lose consciousness and slips forward; he can feel no pain and for a brief moment feels peace. Ryan opens his eyes suddenly and looks around; confused as he feels a soft wind on his face. His eyes begin to clear, enough to see a figure in the distance. He is hopeful and moves toward it. The feel of the sand under his feet tells him that at the very least, he is back on the beach. As the figure gets closer, he sees that it has now begun to run toward him.

"SARA!" Ryan screams as he begins to run toward her.

"Ryan!" he hears Sara call out his name, as she reaches him and they collide and kiss.

"I thought I would never see you again!" Ryan exclaims.

"I missed you so much!" Sara says as they continue to embrace. Ryan looks at Sara, "I love you."

"I love you." Sara replies.

*****

Amber slowly puts her clothes back on as Albert does the same. Their breathing has slowed and they stand there in silence, not knowing what to say. Albert is not sure of what he is feeling, but in the midst of those feelings and emotions he knows that there are some things he has never faced before. Albert in that moment realizes he loves Amber and as he stares at her, he is fixated as Amber's eyes appear to be reflecting that love right back at him.

Albert places his hands around Amber and says, "This is crazy."

Amber gently rubs his arms and agrees, "I know." she says. As the two stand there, the silence is broken by the ringing of the telephone. They are both startled, unsure if Amber should answer it. She hesitates and slowly picks up the receiver and says, "Hello?" Albert looks on curiously as to who might be calling and why. As he watches Albert can sense that the conversation is not going well. Amber has lost all the color to her face and simply says, "Okay, I will be right there." Amber turns and hangs up the receiver, looking at the floor, a single tear runs down her cheek.

"Who was it? What's wrong?" Albert asks.

Amber turns to Albert. "Ryan just tried to commit suicide." she mutters.

"We have to get back to the hospital!" Amber says.

"Of course." Albert replies, "Let's go."

The two quickly race to the hospital and run into the emergency room. Amber sees Dr. Miles, who was Ryan's physician after his accident and coma. Amber runs to him as he turns and recognizes Amber.

"Dr. Miles." she utters. The doctor reaching out and holding onto Amber's arms says,

"Ryan is alive."

As Amber begins to cry, "Can I see him?"

"Not right now, we will let you know when you can, but there is something I have to tell you..."

Amber turns to the doctor, a puzzled look on her face, "Tell me what?" Amber asks.

"Ryan has survived the attempt, but he is in a coma."

"For how long?"

"I don't know," the doctor replies. "I will know more later, but for right now he is alive, and I will let you know if there are any changes. I am so sorry."

Amber turns to Albert. He hugs her and tries to comfort her the best way he can. As they stand there they both are unaware that the staff, who know both of their families, look on in wonder as to why they are together and how their embrace looks to be more than comfort. Suddenly they realize what is happening and while some of the stares they are receiving from the staff are mere curiosity, they know the remaining looks they are getting are certainty, that there is more to them, than just an embrace of comfort.

Amber turns to Albert, "I have to go alone."

Albert smiles, "I know, I'll be right here."

Amber makes her way to the room where Ryan is and paces outside awaiting any word as to when she can see him. As the time slowly moves to the future, Amber is becoming increasingly impatient and begins to ask everyone coming down the hallway or leaving the room when can she can see Ryan. After a few more minutes, Dr. Miles approaches Amber, "You can see him now, but you need to prepare yourself," he cautions. Amber's heart is pounding her body trembling with fear and guilt as she opens the door. She can see Ryan but is unable to recognize him as he is swarmed with tubes and wires. Amber approaches the bed and looks over Ryan, "Why did you do this?" Amber asks softly, as she gently holds Ryan's hand, "Why would you do this?"

While Amber goes to see Ryan, Albert makes his way back to Sara's room; he, too, is hesitant to enter. As he slowly enters the room

Albert makes his way to his normal spot at the edge of Sara's bed. As he sits in the darkness Albert looks toward Sara and his eyes fill with tears. Not for the guilt he feels for what just happened between him and Amber, after all he has done this many times before, but because this is the first time he has ever really felt love. Albert turns toward the door and thinks of what Ryan has done and what Amber must be going through right now. *Life comes down to decisions,* Albert thinks, some decisions you make in your life are good and some not so good but with all that has happened Albert is certain it is the knowingly dangerous decisions that can be the most unforgiving.

CHAPTER
SIXTEEN

Amber finds herself waking up leaning on Ryan's bed, her arm draped over Ryan's leg. As she looks around, it appears that she has been there all night. She looks up at Ryan, *this is not a dream,* she thinks as he is still lying there motionless. The sound of the breathing machine bellowing like a balloon being inflated then deflated over and over again is the only sound that she hears. As she wipes her eyes, she skirmishes, *they hurt, probably from all the crying I've done,* she thinks.

Amber grips Ryan's hand, "I am sorry,…I am so sorry." she says.

She begins to cry, the pain is unbearable as she feels in some way responsible for what has happened. Amber is startled as the doctor enters the room. She quickly composes herself as she is eager to speak with him but hesitant to hear what he might reveal. Amber quickly stands up is nervous and wants answers, but those answers he may not have. The doctor gently places his hand on the back of Amber's arm, Amber looks at him.

"What?" she asks, not knowing what he might say.

The doctor takes a long breath. "Ryan has suffered a hypoxic-anoxic injury as a result of the attempted suicide."

"What is that?" Amber asks, the doctor attempt to answer but Amber quickly interrupts. "What does that mean?"

The doctor pauses, "Anoxia happens when your body or brain completely loses its oxygen supply. Anoxia is usually a result of hypoxia. This means that a part of your body doesn't have enough oxygen."

"Okay, then what is the Hypotic thing?"

The doctor corrects Amber, "Hypoxic. That is when the body is harmed by a lack of oxygen, it's called a hypoxic-anoxic injury. Ryan is in what is called an EEG alpha coma. In medical terms the electroencephalogram (EEG) pattern is characterized by a diffused or widespread rhythmic activity in the alpha frequency band which is typically recorded in patients with profound coma." the doctor says.

"Okay, I am not sure what you said." Amber replies, "What can we do?" Amber ask as her tears begin to stream down her face.

"Right now we are waiting."

"Waiting for what!" Amber screams. "We need to help him!"

The doctor squeezes Amber's arms, "For right now we have done all we can." the doctor replies, "Now it is up to Ryan."

"Up to Ryan, how can it be up to Ryan? You are the doctor!"

"I know this is hard." the doctor says, "We are doing everything humanly possible. I'm very sorry," the doctor turns and begins to walk away.

"Is Ryan going to wake up?" Amber asks as she is holding onto the doctor's lab coat.

"I will not get your hopes up, but there have been a few cases in which the outcome was favorable."

"How many?"

"They are rare."

"How many?" Amber asks again.

"I am personally aware of a survivor who showed an alpha coma after an attempted suicide by hanging, she was a nineteen year old college student."

"What happened to her?"

The doctor hesitant, looking sympathetically not trying to give Amber a false sense of hopes that may not be there.

"Doctor please."

The doctor takes a shallow breath and says, "Okay, she was admitted to the hospital because of respiratory arrest following a hanging attempt, she was found completely pendent. On admission, she was comatose, and the pupils were not reactive to light, Ryan shares some of these same commonalities." the doctor hesitates again.

"Please go on, tell me what happened?"

"I don't want to get too detailed," the doctor replies.

"Please doctor… I want to hear what happened."

The doctor uncomfortable and unwilling to say anymore, tells Amber, "I'm sorry I have to go, I'm sorry," and begins to walk down the hallway.

"At least tell me her name, what was the girls name, can you at least tell me that?" Amber asks, as the doctor walks away. The doctor turns to Amber and says, "Laura…Laura Mills," the doctor mutters as he turns away and walks down the hallway.

Amber looks back at the room where Ryan is, now consumed with finding out more about the girl who survived. Amber approaches the nurses' station to ask if there is a computer she can use. A nurse looking at some charts turns to Amber and says, "Sure, follow me." The nurse leads Amber to a small room where she sees a few chairs and a computer on a small desk in the corner of the room. Amber starts the computer and searches for the name of the girl the doctor gave her. As Amber reads the results and skims over the posting she lands on a portion with details; The young girl's systolic blood pressure was 60 mmHg and immediately an endotracheal intubation was instituted. After six hours from the onset, the spontaneous respiration was restored and the pupils reacted briskly to light. At 48 hours later she was still comatose, presenting flaccid quadriplegia with no responses to stimulations. Amber is not even entirely sure she understands what she is reading but continues on. This alpha rhythm had persisted until seventy-two hours from the onset; slow activity replaced the alpha frequency at one hundred and twenty hours after the attempt. On the 5th hospital day hyperbaric oxygen therapy was given. "Why can't this be an option for Ryan?" she whispers. Amber reads on, now fully involved in the young girls plight. On the 7th day she had become conscious, but showed the apallic syndrome, and on the 45th day the brain MRI revealed diffuse cerebral cortical atrophy, although no lesions were visualized in the brain stem. She showed gradual progress towards neurologic recovery. Amber looks away from the computer screen, remembering the doctor saying that this was his first and only experience of a survivor from alpha coma caused by anoxic encephalopathy following a hanging attempt in twenty-five years. Amber stares in silence clinging to the hope that there may have been more, even though it was his only one. The doctor isn't saying it is not possible or that there is nothing we can do, he is saying we have to be patient and hope that Ryan helps us, Amber says to herself. Amber looks across the room in the direction where Ryan is, "I am so sorry Ryan," she says softly, saddened that she is powerless to do more.

*****

Albert is fidgeting, wondering what is happening. *Where is Amber?* he thinks as he looks out into the hallway. Albert wants to go to Amber; however, he's afraid of what may be said and how it would look. Albert looks at Sara. He begins to feel sad, but this sadness is in a place within his heart he never knew existed, Albert feels remorse not just for what happened between himself and Amber but for all he put Sara through over the years. Albert realizes now, that what is happening is just another layer of pain and is happy Sara is not aware of it. *I can't leave my wife,* Albert thinks, but at the same time he is unable to shake the feeling of being in love with Amber. He feels disgusted with himself; however in a strange way he understands what Amber told him about Ryan's dream. What kind of love would you need to have for someone to leave everything behind to try and find it? *If that is what Ryan was trying to do?* Albert thinks.

*****

Sara smiles as her and Ryan sit along the beach; there are no words that can express how each of them feels being back together again.

"I can't believe I made my way back to you." Ryan says.

"I knew you would come back." Sara says, "I told you, love always finds a way," as she draws a heart in the sand with her name and Ryan's name at its center. Ryan is unsure why, but is wondering as to why he has not dreamt of her. He turns to Sara and asks, "Why do you think we have not been able to see each other?"

Sara continues to stare at the heart she has written in the sand, "I don't know, I have been kind of in and out of here."

"In and out of where?"

"Here on our beach, at our cottage." Ryan just listens intently. "One minute I'm here, then I hear lots of people talking and then I'm not here."

Ryan thinks about what Sara is saying but is unable to offer any answers.

"It's okay." Sara says, "We are here now and that is all that matters," as she turns and looks at Ryan.

Ryan completely agrees and dismisses his concern for the moment as he stares out over the ocean, but inside he is disturbed by her response and for the first time a feeling of fear drapes over him. He knows he has never, up to this point, been afraid while with Sara.

*****

Albert leaves the room and makes his way down the hallway where Ryan's room is located. Albert slowly moves, peering through the open door. He sees Amber sitting at Ryan's side. He thinks for a moment to just walk away, but Amber sees Albert and looks directly at him. Albert knows that she is aware of his presence and moves into the doorway, Amber stands and moves toward the door.

"How are you?" Albert asks.

"I'm okay."

The feeling of not reaching out to each other is like trying to fight gravity, both of them using every ounce of strength they can muster to keep apart. Amber steps out into the hallway. Albert covertly touches Amber's hand as she passes him, and Amber returns the gesture, avoiding being seen. The two of them move down the hallway to the hospital chairs and sit, an open seat between them. The stillness of the hallway is as if someone knows that they are going to be there and wants to make sure they are alone in solitude.

As they sit, Amber stares at the floor and Albert stares at the wall in front of him, both unsure what to think or say. The silence is broken when Albert says to Amber, "I love you."

Amber begins to cry as they both join hands. Amber squeezes Albert's hand without looking up or at him. "How can we do this?" Amber asks.

"I love you." Albert says again.

Amber looks at Albert and says, "I love you too." Amber looks away from him and up to the ceiling, the tears streaming down her face, "Do you know how long I waited for Ryan to love me, and how long I have hoped for the love I feel right now?" Amber looks down at the floor, "I never thought that I would find love without him, now I know that is not true." Albert turns to Amber, the tears streaming down his face. "I found you and even though I don't know what to do now, I am so thankful I did." Albert states, as he is trying to describe to himself what he is feeling.

Suddenly this peaceful and heart-filled moment is shattered as the nursing staff and doctors run into Sara's room. Albert and Amber get to their feet and struggle to understand what is going on, they are both almost to the point of panic, not sure what to do. They both stand, paralyzed as they stare at the commotion unfolding before their eyes. Albert's thoughts immediately go to Sara, *She has died or is dying,* and although he should feel complete sadness he feels relieved. In that moment his mind and heart are in one way devastated, but in another they are relieved as this is one less obstacle he will have to overcome in order to be with Amber. Albert breaks from his thoughts then realizes what kind of person he would have to be to think that?

Albert and Amber race to the room and stand in the doorway. They haven't noticed but they are still holding hands. They watch as the medical staff frantically moving about. Albert's eyes are filled with tears as Amber squeezes his hand, trying to comfort Albert as she realizes how hard it must be no matter what the circumstances now.

"What is going on?" Albert screams. "What is happening?" he screams again as the staff is too busy to respond to his cries.

As Albert looks on, something is wrong with what he and Amber thinks is happening. His eyes glaze at the EKG machine and it is showing a heartbeat. "If she is dead, why is the machine showing life?" he says to Amber. She offers no response and continues to just stare ahead, Albert looks back at the bed and is started as he thinks he sees Sara's hand move. That's not right he thinks as he shakes his head, his mind unable to process what is happening.

In the midst of all the commotion, one of the doctors breaks from the huddle and approaches Albert and Amber who recognizes that it is Dr. Miles "She's awake." Dr. Miles says.

"Awake?" Albert replies, a strange puzzled look on his face.

"Yes she has come out of her coma!" Dr. Miles says elated. Amber releases Albert's hand as she tries to process what the doctor is saying. "We are not sure, but it looks like she is awake and aware. I will let you know more once we run some tests," the doctor says and hurries back to Sara's bedside.

Awake? Albert says to himself again as Amber slowly lowers her head and leaves the room.

At that very moment, Ryan and Sara are walking into the cottage. Ryan is so happy to be back, but thinks of how he got here and feels sadness as he can only imagine what Amber is going through. Suddenly Sara staggers and clutches her chest as she stumbles forward. Ryan races to her as she falls to the floor gasping for air.

"What is happening to me?" Sara asks, the panic in her voice daunting. "Don't let them take me, please, Ryan! Don't let them take me!"

"Take you, who?... I don't know what to do!" Ryan says, "Sara, what do I do?" Ryan asks as the same panic Sara is experiencing begins settling upon him. "I don't know what to do, tell me what to do!" Ryan screams as he holds Sara in his arms her body limp as if her very soul had been removed, their eyes locked together. He pleads with Sara, "Hold on, please, hold on! Don't leave me...Somebody help me! ...somebody help me, please!"

Ryan can feel that Sara has stopped moving as he watches her eyes slowly close, Ryan looks away, he knows Sara is not dying but is leaving all the same. Ryan closes his eyes as he hears Sara trying to say something, Ryan looks down at Sara.

"I love you." Sara whispers.

"Sara, no…no…no, please, Sara, stay with me, please. Oh God…oh God, no…no!" Ryan screams as Sara fades from view, her body like a smoke vapor as Ryan desperately tries to hold on.

He sits on the floor in the now empty room without Sara and looks around at all that remains…the love he felt and the times they shared. Ryan stares down at the floor rubbing it as if she was still there. It is in this moment that everything that has happened becomes crystal clear. From the beach to the cottage, the unusual figurine, smells and most importantly the sign with Love Will Find a Way. *She is back in the world,* Ryan thinks, happy *she is okay and maybe just maybe he thinks, she will dream about me.*

*****

Albert turns and quickly goes after Amber who is in the hallway, a strange look of hollowness in her eyes.

"Amber." Albert says.

Amber looks to Albert. "You have to go home now." Amber whispers.

"But what about us?"

"There is no us, Sara needs you now."

"But I need you."

Amber reaches for Albert's hand and lovingly presses it against her face, she pulls Albert close and kisses him on the cheek.

"Amber." Albert whispers as Amber pulls away, their hands holding on as long as they can. He watches as she makes her way to Ryan's room.

Amber pauses and they both share one final look of love before Amber enters the room. She walks to where Ryan is laying, the sound of the machine helping him breathe is the only sound that can be heard. Amber stands over Ryan as she clutches his hand. Amber looks up at the ceiling and thinks of how unfair it is to have wanted a love she could never receive and now a love she can never have. Amber leans over and kisses Ryan on the forehead and whispers, "I love you." Albert stares down the hallway; he looks to where the staff is still gathered around Sara then turns back to the room where Amber is. He looks up at the ceiling, takes a breath, and goes back into Sara's room.

Sara is awake and looking up at the ceiling. She feels she is unable to speak but knows where she is. *Ryan*, she thinks as a tear leaves her eye. She tilts her head slightly and sees Albert, confirmation that she is right. Albert sees Sara is looking at him and moves to stand beside her and takes her hand.

"Hey, sweetheart." Albert says, the tears streaming down his face, not just happiness for Sara but the sadness of losing Amber.

Sara turns back to the ceiling as the staff hover over her, "I am sorry, please, forgive me." she whispers.

Albert leans in and says, "Forgive you for what?—You don't need to apologize." Albert unaware the apology was not meant for him.

The world seems quieter now, Ryan is still sitting on the floor of the cottage, a mix of feeling both sadness and regret not for the life he lost but for the love he no longer has. Amber stands staring at Ryan forced to accept that she must now go on without Albert and stand by Ryan who may never return. Albert holds Sara's hand wishing it was Amber, he knows that even though he does not believe in karma it is more likely than not that he is getting what he deserves. Sara stares up at the ceiling knowing that Ryan is gone and that the man now at her side would never take his place. Her only thought is how unfair all of this is and what did she ever do to deserve this? In the end, Ryan, Sara, Albert, and Amber find themselves with several things in common; each of them is now in a place they never thought was possible. Each of them found love but were unable to keep it, but most importantly, they all realize that it is not what you do when you find love or it finds you. It is the gratitude you must feel that you were once one of the lucky ones who actually had the honor of experiencing it and why it is so important that if you find love or it finds you, you realize and understand that no matter how short or how long love stays, it will be worth whatever price you had to pay when you had it.

Where does love live? In our hearts, in our minds, or somewhere else? Does love seek us out when we are lost or abandon us when it's necessary? Is love everything we have been led to believe, or is it something we only dream about?

THE END

ABOUT THE AUTHOR

Antonio DeMarco was born in Grants, New Mexico, in 1968. He graduated high school in 1985 then went on to working in the security industry for the next twenty years. At the age of forty-eight, Antonio was inspired to follow a lifelong dream of becoming an artist or writer, which was something he was always passionate about but was never able to pursue or believed could be a possibility. Antonio now lives in Phoenix, Arizona, where he lives with his wife and continues to write and follow his dream.